For:

My mother Kathyrn "Kathi" Wood
My father William "Bill" or "Ace" Hyden
My uncle Robert "UB" or "Bob-a-Louie" Hyden

Continue Resting in Peace. I love and miss you all.

TABLE OF CONTENTS

These 11 short stories are not required to be read in chronological order, however for the best experience it is recommended.

Please share your thoughts (Good or Bad, but hopefully good) and which story you enjoyed the best by contacting me at lancehyden@gmail.com or AuthorLanceHyden on Facebook or writing a review on my author's page on Amazon.com.

Enjoy and Thank you!

ACKNOWLEDGEMENTS

My great supporters-
- Friends, family, and strangers that purchased copies of my previous 2 novels.

My grand supporters-
- The ones that actually read the 2 novels.

My future supporters-
- The ones that will purchase copies of this novel and/or the other 2.

My non-supporters-
- Friends, family, and strangers that have yet to purchase any of my novels. I will win you over eventually (insert diabolical laugh here).

My behind-the-scenes supporters-
- Deb Hyden (Wife, muse, editor, sexy vixen)
- Scott Lange (Bestie, editor, writer, format king).
- Nathan Hyden (Cuz, cover designing God, kool kat).
- Laurie Bell (Great friend, neighbor, eyes, photographer of me).
- Rusty (Family dog, walking partner, slobberer, buddy)

My distributing supporters-
- Sid & Tara Anderson (Great friends, idea-boards, foodies, transporters of my novels to multiple countries).

My creative supporters-
- Zen Leaf dispensary and Sour Sensi Stripes Gelatin Gummies
- WFA music play list
- iPhone notepad

My inspirational supporters (for this book)-
- Live sporting events.
- Michigan/OSU rivalry game (Go Blue)
- College Football, College Basketball (March Madness)
- NHL, NFL, Formula 1, Bowling, Axe Throwing, racing.

- ESPN, Fox Sports, CBS Sports, NFL Network, NHL Network.

My secret supporters-
- James Cameron (Legendary film maker, owner of my first 2 novels).
- Rich Robles (Marine brutha, motivator, reason James Cameron has my novels on his coffee table in New Zealand waiting to be read and turned into box office hits. Wink! Wink! Hint! Hint!).

My supporting teams-
- Detroit Lions (Our time is near)
- Detroit Red Wings (LGRW, return to glory)
- Detroit Tigers (Restore the roar)
- Detroit Pistons (Bring back the Bad Boys)
- Michigan Wolverines (2023 National Champs, alleged sign stealers)

My supporting cast-
- The Lucky Bastards that got characters named after them in this novel- Sid and Tara Anderson, Laurie Bell, David and Ashley Lundberg, Christian Harding, Scottie Brown, Ben Evans, Preston Hyden, Felipe Ramirez and Dave R, Paul and Jen Farabaugh, Mike Pifer, Scott and Becky Lange, Rich Robles, Roberto Taylor, Chef Adam Allison, Jose Cardenas, Dan White, Rafat Zeineddine, Kreg Bahm, Corona Hoang, Trino Orta, Peter Phillips, Ramona Green, Amer Noueihed, Robert Hyden, and William Hyden. Special appearance by Matthew Larson as Hurricane Matthew.

My fun supporters-
- Hyden Hideawayers (friends, family, and partiers)
- Las Vegas- (Sin City, 2nd home, desert oasis)

FOREWORD

After Lance's first two books, I assumed I was the go-to guy for his forewords. Imagine my disappointment in learning I was the second choice to the great and powerful James Cameron. Yes! That James Cameron of Terminator and Avatar fame. How realistic is that? He's a pretty busy guy, and tough to get in touch with, I work for beer. You would not have to hide in the bushes outside my house, stalk me at restaurants, or disguise yourself as a cosplay Navi and sneak onto movie sets to get my attention. You could've avoided that entire legal battle, the restraining order, and that 72-hour psych hold at the State hospital. I'm sorry you discovered Nurse Ratched is a real person. But hey, lessons learned and I'm cool being second fiddle to James Cameron.

Lance and I share a similar love of sports. We both cheer for teams mired in mediocrity and/or annual disappointment. But that is what can make sports great. There is always next year. Talegate is a sports book from an unfamiliar perspective, yet still reveals a love for the game.

We as humans have a romantic attachment to sports which can be difficult to explain. There is a connection between the athletes and the teams they play for. We marvel at their athleticism and flair for the dramatic. Whether it's draining a clutch three-pointer at the buzzer or a dramatic home run in the bottom of the ninth with two outs and the bases loaded to walk off the diamond with a miraculous win, our attention is grasped on every play. Sports can capture our imagination like no other form of entertainment. It's unpredictable. Unfortunately, sports are also unpredictable off the playing field as well.

While gifted with incredible athleticism, commitment to their craft, and dedication and drive to greatness, athletes are still fallible human beings just like the rest of us. As fans, it's easy for us to sit back on our couch and say I don't understand why they abuse drugs or beat women, they have so much going for them. On-field shortcomings can be made up on the next play or the next game. It's our love for the game that gives athletes a hall pass. There is always next season.

Missteps off the field are not the same. These are the transgressions that crumble the metaphorical pedestal we place athletes on. With every Hail Mary pass to win a game there are countless accounts of careers lost to domestic violence. We will always have buzzer-beaters lost to the buzz of the next high of drug or alcohol abuse. The crack of the bat is lost to the crack of the pipe. In sports when the mighty fall, it can be felt by all.

The 1919 Black Sox Scandal was one of the first to break the collective hearts of fans. That season the Chicago White Sox were accused of fixing the most sacred of sacred sporting events, The World Series. For all the kids out there, this was a time without the NFL or the NBA. Baseball was the sport of the Gods and Shoeless Joe Jackson was a god among men. The greatest player of the greatest game in the sport's finest moment was accused of compromising the integrity of the game.

Say it ain't so Joe!

Many will argue Shoeless Joe's innocence to this day, but his lifetime ban from baseball remains.

Gambling and baseball have an unfortunate connection. 1989 another head fell from baseball's Rushmore when Pete Rose received a lifetime ban for betting on baseball games. Being the competitor he was, he only bet on his own team to win.

Parley Hustle!

In 1994 Tonya Harding wanted to represent the United States so badly in the Olympics, that she paid poorly equipped hitmen to help her out. Ex-husband Jeff Gillooly hired meathead thug Shane Stant to take out her only competition Nancy Kerrigan at the knees. He did just that.

Why! Why! Why!

Eventually, Harding served 3 years of probation and received a $160,000 fine.

Professional cycling existed as a fringe sport until Lance Armstrong went into high gear and burst onto the scene in the late 1990s. Armstrong would first capture the sports fans in

1996 when beat cancer and returned to dominating races. We all love the underdog story. He would go on to dominate the sport winning the prestigious Tour de France a record seven times in a row from 1999-2005. Even a cancer survivor cannot overcome a steroid scandal. All of Armstrong's wins and records were vacated by the cycling governing body.

Livestrong Lance. Livestrong!

The National Football League has had its share of scandals. Spygate, Bountygate, and Deflategate. In 2007 the mighty New England Patriots were embroiled in a scandal of using technology to steal the coded play-calling signs of their opponents. In the end, the NFL fined Coach Bill Belichick $500,000, the Patriots $250,000, and a first-round pick.

Bountygate was far more nefarious. In 2012 several members of the New Orleans Saints coaching staff were implicated in creating a slush fund to pay bounties to players who injured the other team's top players. The Saints lost draft picks, received a $500,000 fine and several coaches served suspensions, with Head Coach Sean Payton spending a year away from coaching.

Who dat?

Deflategate might be the most ridiculous scandal of all. This scandal reached its height because one of the best was accused, Tom Brady. In the grand scheme of athletes trying to get a competitive edge, this one seems pretty minor. While the Patriots ended up winning the 2015 Super Bowl, the investigation cast a dark cloud over the season. Brady began the 2015 season with a measly four-game suspension for heinous acts of deflating footballs.

Let's GOOO!

Baseball is full of attempts to gain a competitive edge. Gaylord Perry is a Hall of Fame Pitcher and an admitted spitball pitcher. Umpires caught Joe Niekro red-handed during a game with an emery board used to change the grip on the baseball. Then there is the pine tar incident. George Brett hits a go-ahead home run against the Yankees only to have his bat challenged by the opposing manager for being covered with too much pine tar, a sticky substance used to grip the bat better. The umpired

12

overruled the home run, called Brett out, and ended the game as a Yankees win. Brett famously lost his mind in a moment of uncontrollable insanity.

"If you're going to cheat, it's better you don't get caught." -- Yogi Berra

OJ Simpson made the greatest attempt ever at not getting caught, or shall we say, getting away with murder. On June 17, 1994, OJ captured the nation's attention with a low-speed freeway chase trying to escape arrest for the murders of Nicole Simpson and Ron Goldman in a White Ford Bronco. OJ had reached a height most athletes dream of, Heisman Trophy winner, NFL Hall of Fame, sports commentator, celebrity spokesperson, and Hollywood movie star, now accused murderer. The strange thing is OJ's star never really fell. The unprecedented coverage of the trial and his acquittal only cast his star in a different orbit. One so unique, that no fallen athlete has ever come close.

The Juice is Loose!

Not all scandals are created equal as are the athletes embroiled in them. For every Joe Jackson, there is a notorious "cheater" like Gaylord Perry who can reach the Hall of Fame. Every Lance Armstrong has a Tom Brady who won three more Super Bowls after his scandal.

Scandals in sports reveal athletes to be flawed humans just like the rest of us. They make mistakes, they make bad decisions. Sometimes athletes' crimes are judged in the court of public opinion, other times in the court of their peers.

Talegate includes eleven short stories that run the gamut of sports. As a Detroit Lions fan, Lance has a lifetime of sports heartbreaks and waits until next year. Detriot has not been without its share of sports calamities. In 2004, Detroit hosted the Malice in the Palace, when an on-court scuffle turned into a full fledge brawl with fans in the stands. Although Lance's Lions of the Honolulu blue and silver seem to have dodged any significant scandal. So far.

"With honor, you will keep your fame."

Hope you all enjoy Lance's latest creation.

Cheers ~Scott

TAILGATE

College football provides some of the biggest rivalries in sports beyond just the players on the field or court. The students and fans get involved in many creative ways before their rivalry games start. These are primarily innocent pranks, such as Arizona State University painting their school colors, maroon and gold, on the large mountainside "A" on the University of Arizona's campus. Not to be outdone, U of A returned the favor to ASU's large mountainside "A" with blue and red paint. A University of Tennessee fan put his school's team flag in the hands of the Nick Saban statue outside of Bryant-Denny Stadium at the University of Alabama before one of their big games. In 1916, Texas A&M fans branded Bevo, the University of Texas Longhorns living steer mascot, with a "13-0", the score that Texas A&M beat the Longhorns by the previous year.

Minor innocent vandalism, stealing each other's mascots, or elaborate pranks over time have helped shape these rivalries. Occasionally, some fans take it too far and end up on the wrong side of the law. For example, in 2010, a University of Alabama fan, Harvey Updyke, poisoned two large oak trees at Toomer's Corner on the University of Auburn's campus. He would pay a hefty fine and serve jail time.

As part of the "fun," students have placed their sacred statues, landmarks, or mascots under 24-hour security watch before these big games. This makes it difficult for opposing fans to pull off their high jinks, which leads to fans targeting other unprotected areas of the schools.

The University of Florida and Florida State University are only a 2-hour drive apart on the I-10 and I-75, providing short day trips for their student body to travel to games. The student sections in the opposing stadiums are usually well-represented. The battle for the "Florida Cup" is taken seriously between the school's football teams that meet every year towards the end of the season. The game is extra vital this year because both schools are undefeated and vying for a spot in the college football playoffs. The game is at Ben Hill Griffin Stadium on the campus of the University of Florida in Gainesville. However, according to the Las Vegas oddsmakers, FSU is favored to win by 3 ½ points.

The charter bus arrives from the FSU campus in Tallahassee, Florida, with many students ready to cheer their school's team to victory. The driver is Kelvin White, an older black man in his 60s and a lifelong FSU fan. He pulls into the large bus area, where it will sit until it's time to return to Tallahassee after the game's conclusion. Two FSU students on the bus, Trevor Garrison and Chris Moore, are best friends and roommates. They're excited about this historic match-up and quickly exit the bus with the other thrilled students. Trevor has applied his gold, black, and garnet war paint on his face, and Chris is wearing his Seminoles T-shirt and hat. Chris dislikes painting his face because he claims it "makes him break out." The two besties head over to join the tailgate party in the FSU reserved section of the parking lot.

The tailgate section is closed off to only FSU students with tickets. Trevor and Chris get patted down by security and hand over their tickets for entry. The tailgate area is jumping with music, fans' chants, and the buzz of excitement. Numerous footballs are being tossed around, BBQ grills are cooking various meats and food, and a few cornhole games are underway that have turned into drinking games. One game over in the corner, in between two large pickup trucks, has turned into "strip cornhole." The guys encouraged some naïve college girls into playing after a few drinks. The young women either never played before or just really sucked at it because they're all nearly naked and don't seem to care; shots of tequila and whiskey will do that.

Trevor and Chris join some friends who are grilling hot dogs and hamburgers. They become part of the gold and garnet sea mingling on top of the parking lot asphalt until it's time for them to flock into the stadium a couple of hours from now.

Rich Rojas and Alex Thornton had plans to travel to the FSU campus to paint their student kiosk the Gator colors, orange and blue. However, their plans were thwarted by the extra amount of FSU students, surveillance cameras, and security guards monitoring the campus for potential Gator pranksters. Florida State pranksters managed to get 2,000 school-colored balloons into the Florida Gator's head coach's office a few days ago. Rich and Alex swore retaliation against the FSU perpetrators and had a new plan. They decided that game day was their best opportunity to strike.

The section of the parking lot reserved for all tour and school buses is mostly empty of people. A few bus drivers remain inspecting their vehicles before the ride back. Several bus drivers hang out in one of the luxury party buses, watching the game on the big screen. The rest of the drivers have tickets to the game and are inside the stadium. Alex and Rich sit in a black Ford Ranger pickup truck and watch Kelvin leave to join his fellow bus drivers to watch the game. The vacant bus will be the best opportunity to pull off one of the most fantastic and funny college pranks ever. *They will be legends and spoken about for years to come!*

Alex slowly drives the pickup truck towards the FSU tour bus. He pulls up right beside the sliding door and parks. The Ford Ranger is positioned perfectly between two tour buses where nobody can see them. They leave the truck, wearing gloves, and walk to the bus door. Alex pulls on the handle and opens the bus door. Rich made an educated guess that it would be unlocked since there was no reason to lock them. They walk to the pickup's tailgate, open it, and then drag out their *"instruments for hilarities."* They carry the two large items hidden under sheets onto the bus one at a time. Alex mounts the two hidden webcams to record and watch their future TikTok-worthy victims. *"We'll be prank masters and influencers after this, with over 10 million views,"* they tell themselves as Alex drives away from the future prank location.

"Did you seal all the emergency exits so nobody can get out? We don't want someone going through the roof hatch and jumping off the top of the bus or climbing through the windows and breaking their ankle or leg. Somebody could sue us," Alex asks.

"Yes, we're all good. The only way in and out of that bus is the front door. They can't open any of the emergency exits," Rich answers.

"This is going to be epic," Alex says.

Kelvin enters his charter bus to prepare for the students, who will be drunk and excited after the blowout FSU just handed to the University of Florida. He left the luxury tour bus with about 5 minutes left in the game, and FSU was winning 52-17. So, barring an act of God, the game was essentially over. He knew the passengers would slowly return to the bus sporadically in a few more minutes. Some of them like to come back early to avoid crowds exiting the stadium and, to the annoyance of the early arriving students and Kelvin, others like to stay in and around the stadium well after the game to socialize and talk smack to University of Florida fans. Kelvin has a head count of 47 FSU souls and is responsible for returning them to Tallahassee safely.

"He's going to fuck it all up. He'll get scared and tell the passengers they can't get on. Giving us only one scare for TikTok," Alex whines.

"He's just going in to turn on the engine and get the bus ready. He might not even see them. Let it play out, bro," Rich replies.

Kelvin turns the engine on and tries to close the bus door, but he has no luck. He pushes the close button for a third time, and the door remains open.

"Dammit, I have meant to get this door fixed. I can't figure out why it takes several pushes before it opens or closes the door," he complains to himself.

He leaves the door open and walks to the back of the bus to inspect the restroom.

"Well, you're right; he's going to see it now and get the surprise of his life," Rich says, preparing for his prank to work while the two pranksters watch on Rich's iPad.

"Fuck, this sucks. Oh well, maybe it will be a hilarious reaction of an old black guy shitting his pants, which would still get millions of views," Alex hopes.

Kelvin opens the restroom door and is confronted by two young male American alligators. He screams in fright, stumbles backward, and falls between a row of chairs, hitting his head on the armrest.

"Yes! That's fucking hilarious. This will go viral quick," Alex claims.

The alligators are small and fast and want out of that cramped space. They quickly climb on Kelvin and ravenously begin eating his face and torso. His screams fade out as the alligators continue their feast.

Rich and Alex quickly silence their laughs from Kelvin's initial reaction to the reptile's surprise once they witness the horrific death of the elderly bus driver.

"What the fuck just happened? They're not supposed to be fully awake yet. We're in fucking trouble now," Alex states.

"I thought you said they wouldn't attack because they've been fed and drugged?" Rich asks.

"That's how my uncle preps them before putting on a show for his audience so they don't attack him. Fuck, we're going to jail," Alex says, starting to cry.

"No, we're not! We were never here. They can't prove anything without witnesses, and nobody saw us," Rich replies, understanding their trouble level.

"One small problem with that, Rich. All of my uncle's alligators at his farm are FUCKING tagged, named, and tracked," Alex educates.

"Relax, let's go round them up before anybody else arrives, and we'll act like we were never here, or the other option is we'll be charged with murder," Rich says, trying to strike fear into Alex.

"Fuck. Let's do this quick and get them back to my uncle's gator farm," Alex agrees.

Trevor and Chris approach the bus with three other FSU passengers. They're earlier than most because they left the game with a minute remaining. Chris isn't feeling well and just wants to return to the bus and relax. Two of the passengers they arrive with are holding up their drunk female friend. The door to the bus is open and inviting to Chris' eyes.

"Shit! There are some passengers at the door getting ready to get on. We're too late, and now we're going to fucking prison for life," Alex states after seeing them arrive and stops the truck.

They stop about two hundred yards from the bus and watch them on Chris' iPad through the hidden webcams on the bus.

Trevor and Chris are the first to board, with the other three carefully climbing the four steep bus steps to get their drunk friend to "safety."

"Hey Kelvin, you here, buddy? We're back! The games are over, and we won!" Trevor shouts to elicit a response from Kelvin.

"Trevor, what's that in the back?" Chris says, squinting his eyes for better viewing down the dark center bus aisle.

"Oh shit, that's Kelvin. He's down on the ground. Kelvin! Kelvin!" Trevor shouts as he starts running towards him.

Chris races behind to reach Kelvin's motionless body, which is lying in a row of seats close to the back. The two passengers drop their friend in the first open seat at the front, and she passes out. The male passenger walks towards the back to see what's happening. His girlfriend stays standing in the aisle, watching him and her drunk friend.

The male passenger looks at Kelvin, who is a few rows away from his fellow FSU fans. Trevor is the first to reach Kelvin and discovers his face is like chewed-up meat. Chris slips on a puddle of blood and falls into it. His favorite FSU shirt is now blood-soaked.

"Kelvin's been murdered! Don't come back here!" Trevor yells.

"What's going on? Is he okay?" the male passenger asks.

SNAP!

Suddenly, the man's ankles are in the mouth of a ferocious alligator. He falls to the ground in pain and tries kicking the animal frantically to make him release his tight grasp.

His girlfriend screams and falls back into the control panel, hitting the closed-door button that Kelvin tried accomplishing a few minutes ago. It finally works, and the door closes.

The man is lying on his back, still kicking at the alligator, hoping to knock him off and release his ankle. He looks to his right, and the other alligator is silent. They stare at each other for about two seconds before the alligator lunges forward and sinks its numerous conical-shaped teeth into his skull.

The girlfriend is screaming hysterically while lying frozen with fear on the aisle floor and watching her boyfriend become an alligator chew toy. The scream jolts the drunk friend awake for a brief moment.

"Yay! Go Flori Sta…" she shouts, slurring her speech, and passes back out.

Trevor and Chris quickly climb up on the seats to avoid contact with the swamp creatures.

Rich and Alex watch in horror and decide not to help them or call the authorities. Rich is trying to think of a way out of this, and Alex is terrified of what will happen to them.

"I'll think of something, bro, don't worry. Let's go make sure they don't get out," Rich explains.

The girlfriend stops screaming as extreme fright has silenced her after one of the alligators has spotted her and is eerily walking up the aisle. Trevor and Chris are screaming for her to get up and open the door. Trevor begins trying to climb over rows of chairs to reach her before the alligator does, while Chris is trying to distract the other alligator. The girl starts moving, reaches over, and presses the open door, but nothing happens. She tries again, but there is still no movement. The alligator has reached its destination and cautiously crawls up the young woman's stiff legs. She stops trying to press the button and lays very still, hoping that no movement will fool the beast and it will move on.

SNAP!

The alligator latches onto the girlfriend's throat, and blood instantly sprays all over the front windshield and driver's seat. Trevor is still a few rows back and stops climbing after watching her neck crushed by the reptile's mighty jaws.

"Trevor, we have to get out of here. Pop that roof hatch open two aisles ahead of you, and I'll get out the emergency exit window one row behind me," Chris instructs.

"You get out first, I have to get this drunk bitch. I can't leave her in here with these blood-thirsty monsters," Trevor replies.

Chris tries the side-window emergency latch, but the window doesn't open. He tries kicking it, but nothing happens. The sound draws the alligator's attention, and he climbs onto the seat, which Chris quickly vacates.

At the same time, Trevor tries to open the roof hatch, which is also stuck closed. His foot slips off the seat, and he falls to the ground, landing on the alligator's tail. The beast releases his death grip from the girlfriend's throat and quickly turns its attention to Trevor. The alligator snaps his jaws twice at Trevor as it crawls towards him. Trevor notices someone left their backpack on a seat. He grabs and throws it into the alligator's mouth, distracting him long enough to climb back onto the seats.

"What the fuck? Are you okay? I can't get these emergency exits to open," Chris says, panicking.

"That was a close one, but I'm good. Just keep kicking at it, or try another window," Trevor calmly replies.

"Trev, this isn't the best time, but it might be my only chance. In case we don't get out of here, I just wanted to tell you that I've loved you since our first class. I should've said something sooner, but I know you might not feel the same way," Chris reveals.

"I'm so happy to hear you say that. I love you, too. I just wasn't sure you felt the same way about me, and I didn't want to make it weird as roommates if I was wrong," Trevor admits.

Rich and Alex arrive at the side of the bus and stop the truck. They continue to watch the carnage on the iPad. The bus windows are too tinted to see inside. Chris notices the black truck pull up.

"Hey, someone just pulled up on your side of the bus. Knock on the window for help," Chris tells Trevor.

Trevor and Chris start pounding on the window, but they notice the two guys in the truck just sitting there watching something on an iPad. Trevor squints his eyes and can tell they're watching what's happening on the bus. He can't see their faces but notices a long alligator tattoo on one of the men's arms.

"Chris, I think they're the motherfuckers that did this. They're watching us. Look, there's a webcam mounted on the ceiling, and another one is upfront. Can you get to that one and rip it off?" Trevor discovers.

Both of the men reach the webcams and yank them off the ceiling. They smash them on the bus floor. Rich and Alex jump at the surprise of being discovered.

"Fuck, we're busted! We have to let them out and tell the police everything. It was just a prank gone wrong," Alex says.

"Fuck that, new plan. Your uncle's out of town, so he could say someone stole the truck and the gators to do this. We were never here. We'll ditch the truck a few miles out of town. Let's go!" Rich commands.

"They just left. Fucking murderers," Chris says.

Trevor scans the entire bus, looking for a way out. A few years ago, after looking over a safety card on a previous tour bus, he suddenly remembered that all tour buses' front windshields could be kicked out from the inside as an emergency exit.

"Chris, meet me at the front of the bus. I know how to get us out of here," Trevor instructs.

One of the alligators stays still next to the dead man's body, watching Chris' movements. The other alligator has managed to get stuck down the steep stairs at the front bus door. Trevor realizes this is the best time to jump down and kick the windshield.

After five kicks, the windshield falls entirely out of the bus. Chris is a few rows past the alligator, so he jumps into the aisle and runs up to the front of the bus. He grabs the drunk girl and carries her to the window. She briefly awakens again and sees an alligator approaching them from behind.

"Fuck you, Gators, we beat you..." she tries to say but ends up puking on the alligator's head as he is about to bite down at Chris' leg.

"Oh shit! I didn't notice that fucker was this close. Trevor, climb out, and I'll throw her to you." Chris says.

Trevor jumps out of the bus and waits for Chris to toss the small, drunk FSU girl to safety. The first alligator violently tries to escape the stairwell but remains stuck. The other alligator is blinded by the large amounts of tequila-based puke covering its eyes and head. Chris gently tosses the girl to Trevor and then hops out of the bus. A couple of drivers and several fans run over to the survivors after hearing the windshield crashing to the ground.

About 15 minutes after their escape, Trevor and Chris sit on a couple of camping chairs that someone provided. They explain what happened to the police and animal control authorities. They give the name on the side of the black truck with the two men in it... *Frank's Gator Farm and Zoo*. However, Trevor leaves out one critical detail: the alligator arm tattoo.

Two months later.

Trevor and Chris are in their college dorm room, snuggled on the couch and watching the local evening news.

"I'm so happy you're back from your trip. It was lonely here the last three days," Chris says before a breaking news alert interrupts him.

"There were two bodies discovered in the alligator ponds at *Frank's Gator Farm and Zoo* today in Gainesville, just a few miles outside of the University of Florida's campus. You'll recall this farm is a part of an ongoing investigation into the FSU tour bus alligator attack a couple of months ago. The owner, Frank Thornton, was cleared of the incident. He was out of town and claimed his truck and alligators were stolen. The bodies aren't officially identified, but sources say that a long alligator tattoo on the arm of one of the victims helped identify the body of Alex Thornton, the owner's nephew. Alex and his FSU fraternity brother, Rich Rojas, have been missing for three days and are both still considered suspects in the investigation," The journalist reports live from *Frank's Gator Farm and Zoo*.

"Wow, Karma served bitches! I hope it's those murderous pieces of shit that killed poor Kelvin and that couple. Too bad we couldn't identify their faces from the bus window," Chris states.

"Yeah, it was too dark. I could only see the iPad screen. Hey, the silver lining is that it finally brought us together," Trevor replies.

"I wonder if the uncle killed them out of anger for using his gators and truck?" Chris speculates.

Trevor pulls Chris in tighter for a hug. " Yeah, I'm sure that's what happened, babe," he says with a satisfying smile.

DIERS FOR FLYERS

One of the most significant sports towns in the United States is "The City of Brotherly Love," Philadelphia, Pennsylvania. However, if you have ever attended any of their major sporting events as a fan of the visiting team, "Brotherly Love" is the last thing you think of. The Eagles, Phillies, 76ers, and Flyer's fan bases are often ridiculed by their rival team's devotees. The Philly faithful are among the most passionate, loyal, and knowledgeable in sports, and they're not afraid for everyone to know it... This is why Philly fans lead the way in numerous sports polls taken by opposing fans and players as the "Most Hated Fans in Sports."

The latest Philly teams that provided the city with a championship title and parade were the 2018 Philadelphia Eagles and the 2008 Phillies, which briefly quenched the city's thirst for a championship. The Philadelphia 76ers basketball team last tasted NBA championship glory in 1983, over 40 years ago. However, the Philadelphia Flyers in the NHL have struggled to win that coveted Stanley Cup since the 1975 season, which is currently the 4th longest drought in the NHL. A passionate fan base in a sports town like Philly, hungry for an NHL title, can be annoying if you're not one of them. Their hatred for the opposing team and lack of a championship is a recipe for anger and hate and produces the "City of Step-Brotherly Hate."

The Flyers are going into their 4th year of a complete rebuild and have one of the youngest teams in the NHL. The addition of a few veteran free agents during the off-season, combined with the youth of this team, has the city hopeful for at least a playoff berth this season. They missed the playoffs last season by only a few points. The Flyer's organization believes their additions of skilled veteran players, more experience from the younger players, and their new head coach and Philly native, Ike "The Enforcer" Flowers, will elevate them into the playoffs and possibly a date with Lord Stanley's Cup. Their first test is tonight, the home and season opener, against their rivals and one of the NHL's original six, the New York Rangers.

Homicide detective Kreg "with a K" Lahm has been a Philly cop for 24 years and is considering retiring in the next year or two. Detective Lahm started his police career after serving four years as a military policeman in the United States Army. His experience as an MP was an easy transition into civilian law enforcement, but that doesn't mean Kreg "with a K" didn't have other dreams or ambitions.

He's always wanted to own a bar, like on his favorite TV shows, "Cheers" and "Always Sunny in Philadelphia." In fact, when he fulfills that dream and opens his bar, he's already got a couple of names picked out. His first and favorite option is a tribute to those two hilarious and iconic sitcoms, "Cheers to Paddy's Pub." He's also a massive "Star Wars" fan; his birthday is May 4th, and he loves telling everyone, "May the 4th be with you!". His all-time favorite character from the space saga is *Baby Yoda.* So*,* the second option is "Gin Grogu," a playful spin-off of *Baby Yoda's* real name, "Din Grogu," in the Disney+ hit series, "The Mandalorian."

Detective Lahm sits comfortably at his desk, reviewing paperwork from a case he just closed. His captain walks up and hands him a note with a location.

"Got a fresh one for you, Lahm. Someone didn't take the Flyers season opener loss last night very well. For 20 years, I've been a season ticket holder of this fucking team; it's getting too expensive to watch them lose year after year. This is my last year getting tickets," Captain Bernie Miller informs.

"Fuck! Did another stupid Flyer fan go too far in a drunken fight and kill a Rangers fan again? This is why we get a bad rap as Philly fans," Detective Lahm responds.

"I don't think so; it's the Philly fan who's dead," the captain answers as he walks back to his office.

Detective Lahm grabs his jacket from the back of his desk chair and departs to the homicide location provided by his superior. On the way out, he snatches a glazed donut from the box of *Federal Donuts* sitting on the desk belonging to homicide detective Torino Ortez, who is curiously absent from his desk, Lahm notices.

Detective Lahm approaches the body, and it's covered in blood. The face was beaten so severely that it made the corpse unrecognizable. He was wearing a #88 *Eric Lindros* Flyer jersey that was blood-soaked. Detective Lahm notices a medical kit belonging to the Medical Examiner, Dr. Korona Huang, sitting beside the victim. She has already arrived before him.

The uniformed police had already roped off the crime scene where the victim was discovered. The body was propped up in a sitting position against the brick wall of *Sticks Sports Bar*, just a couple miles away from the *Wells Fargo Center*, the home of the Philadelphia Flyers.

"Hey, I'm Detective Kreg, with a K, Lahm. Who discovered the body and called it in? What time did that happen?" Detective Lahm asks while showing his badge to a uniformed police officer watching over the body.

"Yes, sir, it's the gentleman my partner is interviewing there. The witness is a jogger out early for his morning run and stumbled across the body around 530am this morning, sir," the officer replies, pointing in the direction of his partner and the witness.

As he's looking at the body, Detective Lahm notices something wedged in the victim's mouth. He kneels, puts on his latex gloves, and extracts the object from the mouth. The item is a replica NHL hockey puck with the Flyer's logo on top and a folded-up piece of paper taped to it on the opposite side. He peels it off and begins to unfold it as Dr. Korona Huang approaches carrying another piece of equipment. He thinks she's attractive but finds her annoying and inappropriate. They're around the same age and both single. It's no secret around the station that Dr. Huang has a crush on Detective Lahm and constantly calls him cute little pet names.

"What 'cha got there, Lamb Sandwich?" She asks with a flirty tone, using his least favorite of those cute little pet names.

"Found this note attached to the hockey puck that was shoved into his mouth by the killer," Detective Lahm responds, slightly annoyed.

"Does it say, Detective Lamb, will you go to the police ball with me? Circle yes or no," she says jokingly but with an innuendo for the upcoming Philadelphia Policeman's Ball.

"No, Dr. Huang, it's not a high school love note. It's a poem by the killer!" He replies, clearly not in the mood for jokes.

A losing hockey team I can take no more,
A new body every time they have a lower score.
No stoppage of games; they must continue to play,
Or I will find more victims to slay.

"Well, he's no Robert Frost," Dr. Huang quips.

"No, but I don't think he's going to stop. This is the first of many unless the Flyers can win or we find him quickly. And it's only the first game of the season," Kreg says, staring down at this killer's first victim.

"A murder for every Flyer's loss this season? I guess we'll be busy and seeing much more of each other 'Rack of Lamb,'" Korona states.

Detective Lahm rolls his eyes and doesn't bother telling her for the thousandth time that, *It's pronounced La-hm, not fucking Lamb.*

Kevin McMillan and his friends are huge sports fans who often watch their favorite Philadelphia team play at *Overtime's Sports Bar and Grill* (Home of the third-best Philly Sandwich in town). Kevin and his three buddies are sitting at a tabletop in the center of the bar, watching the Flyer's second game of the season. They're on the road playing the Buffalo Sabres, and the game is in the final minutes of the third period, with Philadelphia down by one goal.

"For fuck's sake, we better not lose to the shitty Sabres!" Kevin yells out.

One of the Sabres players trips the Flyer's star center, Stefan "Hobby" Hobelchek, and draws a penalty with 1:28 left to play. Everyone in the bar cheers.

"That's what I'm fucking talking about, Hobby! He's the best fucking player in the league!" Kevin claims.

The bar is loud, and everyone is cheering for the Flyers to score a power play goal to tie it up. With less than a minute left, Coach Ike Flowers pulls the goalie to make it a 6 on 4 advantage. This leaves their net empty and exposed for the Sabres, a strategy all 31 NHL teams would implement.

CLANK!

"Hobby, you fucking bum!" Kevin shouts as the puck hits the crossbar and stays out of the net from a slap shot by Kevin's favorite player, Hobelchek.

The puck finds its way to a Buffalo defenseman, who blindly swats his hockey stick to clear it down the ice. By luck, it finds the empty net, and the red light signaling a goal goes off, with Buffalo fans going crazy in the arena. Final: Buffalo 4 Philadelphia 2.

"Alright, Kev, we're outta here, bro. We'll get the next one on Friday night back here at home," one of Kevin's buddies says.

"These fucking clowns better fucking win. Can't go down 0-3 to start the fucking season. I'm staying for another beer to drown my fucking frustration. I'll see you guys here on fucking Friday," Kevin says, dropping numerous "F" bombs every time he's drunk and pissed off.

The three friends throw some money on the table for their portion of the bill and walk out of the bar. Kevin waves over the waitress and orders another "Hopdevil IPA", a Philadelphia favorite.

"Tough loss, man. This team is better than that. We should be 2-0 right now," An older man sitting at the table next to Kevin says.

He's wearing a Flyer's ball cap, a black Flyer's hoodie sweatshirt, and blue jeans. He's sitting alone, and Kevin thinks, *I didn't even notice this guy sitting here the whole game.*

"Yeah, this is a fucking poor start, and I'm already worried about this fucking team. We need a trip to the fucking playoffs this year," Kevin replies.

"Let me get this round, brutha," the man offers.

He joins Kevin at his table, and the two men continue to talk about the Flyers and what they would do to improve the team. The typical beer-drinking bar-room "If I were the team's General Manager..." sports fan comments that every city has, and Kevin is one of the best. *If the Flyer's organization listened to him, they would win the Stanley Cup every season.*

Detective Lahm turns on his car radio to "The John Kincade Show," a popular sports talk show on WPEN 97.5FM. It is his usual "go-to listening" for his morning commute to the station. John Kincade is talking about the Flyers' game last night with his producer and sidekick, Mick Van Dusen, better known as MVD, who was a former rapper for a boy band in the 90s called "The Philly Boyz."

"Well, the Flyers lost a heartbreaker last night to the Sabres, the worst team in the league last year. This is a bad start for our boys in burnt orange, black, and white," John Kincade reports.

"I'm sick of the losing, and I'm not the only fan. I've lived in this beautiful city my whole life span. 47 years and haven't watched the Flyers raise the cup yet, and most of the seasons I just want to forget," MVD speaks in a rhyming fashion, making him popular with the listeners.

Detective Lahm chuckles at MVD's rhyme as he exits his vehicle. He sees Dr. Huang already at the scene and looking over the body that is behind a dumpster in an alley somewhere in downtown Philadelphia. The alleys all just blend in after time for Detective Lahm; he's seen so many bodies in them over the years, a popular killing field. He always wonders, *If we didn't have alleys, would there still be this many murders.*

"Hey Bam Bam Lamb, how are you gorgeous?" Dr. Huang greets Kreg.

"I'm fine. What do we have this time? Judging by the bloody Flyer's jersey, another victim from last night's loss," he makes an educated guess.

"You got it, Lamb chops. Killed the same way as the first victim. There are several lacerations from a beating to the face, with a hockey puck and note wedged into his mouth," Dr. Huang informs.

"Great. Another shitty poem. Let me read it, please," he says, holding his hand out for Dr. Huang to place the folded note.

O for 2 to start the season,
Every loss gives me a reason.
Last night's loss to the Sabres,
Resulting in the loss of one of our friendly neighbors.

Detective Lahm bends down and pulls out the wallet from the dead man's back pocket to identify the poor soul. The driver's license reads Kevin McMillan, age 38, 5'10", brown hair, brown eyes.

"It's just a matter of time before the media gets wind of this and gives this sick fuck a stupid nickname." Detective Lahm states.

"You mean like 'The Stanley Cut,' or how about 'Slab Shot'? Oh wait, I got it, 'The Ghoulie'! You know, like the goalie. You get it?" Dr. Huang adds.

"Yeah, I got it. Please stop," he replies.

Three months later, Coach Ike "The Enforcer" Flowers arrives at the podium for his post-game press conference with the media. He rarely looks like he's in a good mood, but after tonight's big victory and 5th win in a row, he actually looks happy.

"Coach Flowers, what has the team playing so well the past couple of months to move into 2nd place?" reporter one asks.

"After a poor start to the season, we've finally put it all together with hard work and determination. The men are giving 110% and having fun out there," the coach answers.

"Do you think 'The Philly Poet' murders have any motivation for the players to perform better to save lives?" Reporter two asks.

"Fuck no. These guys are playing hard for themselves, the team, and the city. It's unfair for the media and fans to put that added pressure on them; they're not heroes; they play hockey! I tell them every game, play in the now and not for what might happen after!" he replies with passion and frustration.

"Well, there's a lot of fans, people in the media, and even a few players that believe 'The Philly Poet' has something to do with the winning. Many people, including me, don't want him caught just yet," Reporter one admits.

"That's just fucking silly and stupid. If I hear one of my players say these killings are a good thing, they'll be a healthy scratch for the rest of the season. And you, sir, can consider yourself banned from my press conferences from this point on!" the Coach says, visibly angry and no longer carrying that rare smile.

"I don't think you can ban me from press conferences, coach. I meant no disrespect. I'm stating what the people are saying. We all want the winning to continue, so there are no more murders," Reporter One replies.

"Unfortunately, we can't win every fucking game. We just have to let the police do their jobs and hope they catch this crazy son-of-a-bitch," the coach states.

"Coach Ike, your college major was American Poetry at Notre Dame; how do you rate 'The Philly Poet's' work that's been leaked to the media?" a third reporter asks.

"Dog shit!" He says, abruptly leaving the podium and ending the press conference.

Detective Lahm hesitates to look at the ESPN app on his phone to see the Flyer's score last night. They played the first-place Detroit Red Wings and were losing 1-0 after the 1st period when the detective fell asleep in his favorite chair. He's sitting in the car, pulls a cell phone out of his pocket, and opens the ESPN app to view last night's NHL scores... 5-0 Detroit over Philadelphia, ending the Flyer's 5-game winning streak. He knows it's just a matter of time before his phone rings, and he's given the location of the "Philly Poet's" next victim. A moniker he disapproved of, but the media ran with it, and the city has embraced it. He puts the phone down and backs out of the driveway to begin his 20-minute commute to the station.

"Don't get too comfortable, Lahm; we got fresh ones downtown. The 'Poet' has struck again after last night's embarrassing loss to the fucking 'Dead Wings,' and he's clearly not happy about it," Captain Miller says as Detective Lahm enters the room to start his shift.

"Did you say fresh ones, as in plural?" Detective Lahm asks.

"Like I said, the 'Poet' isn't happy about this loss. Dr. Huang is already on site. Go see what she's found out," the captain orders.

Detective Lahm turns around and heads out the door, not even stopping by his desk, which was only 20 feet away. However, Detective Torino's desk is on the way out, and the fresh *Starbucks* coffee he left while attending a meeting in the conference room now belongs to Detective Lahm.

"Well, it's about time you got here. Lamb and cheese sandwich, now it's a foursome," Dr. Huang jokes while examining the two gruesome bodies.

"What do we have here, Dr. Huang? Looks like a possible married couple," he asks, looking down at the man and woman's corpse.

"Yeah, it's so romantic how the killer positioned them. It reminds me of the old couple in Titanic cuddling in bed together while accepting their fate. It made me cry. We should cuddle and watch Titanic tonight, then maybe some 'Wham Bam, thank you, Lamb,'" Dr. Huang suggests.

"Seriously, Dr. Huang, please keep this professional; this isn't a joking matter. That poor couple's lives ended over a stupid hockey game loss. They're the 9th and 10th victim of the season. We have to catch this son-of-a-bitch!" Detective Lahm replies with evident frustration.

"Don't worry, Lamb Stew. We will find him or her. Let's not rule out that it's a woman. We have some good evidence and leads to follow up on. I feel like we're close. Here are the next two poems that I've extracted from their mouths," she informs the detective.

"Okay, let's see what shitty Eminem has to say," he replies.

"Shitty Eminem, you're so funny, Lamb Kebab. The first note was in the man's mouth, and the second was in her mouth. Mmm, all these things in people's mouths have me thinking," Dr. Huang says suggestively.

"Well, don't!" Detective Lamb says.

His mouth:
The Flyer's winning streak ended,
Just like the lives of this couple that I befriended.
Losing to the dreaded team from Detroit,
Their deaths I had to exploit.

Her mouth:
With the playoffs approaching and in sight,
I hope the team will continue to fight.
I prefer that I don't have to kill anymore,
Only winning the cup will close that door.

"We know he hates the Red Wings more than the other teams we've lost against. We know he's an older gentleman, probably in his 50s or 60s, white, and in good shape," Detective Lahm thinks out loud.

"Did I ever tell you I lived in Detroit for a couple years with my ex, who was a songwriter? He turned out to be a cheating prick, nearly ruining my life. Anyway, honey-baked Lamb, why do you say our killer is a white man and older?" Dr. Huang asks.

"Because only a Flyer's fan that has lived through so many years of losing would resort to killing for Philly to win the cup. A younger man hasn't lived long enough to feel this much disappointment. As for him being white, I'm just playing the odds of the hockey demographics. Although this is the wrong way to go about it, I can understand why he does it," he answers.

"You da man, Moon's over my Lammy! See, I told you we were getting closer. But it still could be an older woman," Dr. Huang replies.

"Doubtful. However, I won't rule that out just yet," he says.

The Flyer's regular season is ending with only one game remaining. Their record is 52 wins, 18 losses, and 12 overtime losses. They're sitting in first place in the Metropolitan division of the Eastern Conference, earning their way to the playoffs as the number one seed. Those 18 losses have resulted in 19 deaths by the "Philly Poet," the one extra death because of the couple that was killed after the Detroit game. The killer sent a poem to *The Philadelphia Inquirer* stating he would not kill for overtime losses since the team still earns a point for those games. The fans and media consider this a noble gesture, and it somehow turned him into a local hero in many Philadelphians' eyes.

The city of Philadelphia is buzzing with their team's performance this season, and many people are now giving enormous credit to the "Philly Poet." Detective Lahm is not one of those people. He's still on the case and compiling a list of his top suspects. He's driving to the station and sees a billboard that reads: "Dear Police, please find the 'Philly Poet' after the Playoffs. Sincerely, the fans."

"You've got to be fucking kidding me. What the hell is wrong with people?" He asks himself.

He decides to turn on the sports talk radio program for the remainder of his journey to work. The host is talking about the last Flyers game of the regular season tonight at home against the New Jersey Devils, who are in last place and not going to the playoffs.

"It looks like coach Flowers has decided to sit some of the stars tonight to rest them for round one of the playoffs against the wild-card New York Islanders. MVD has left the booth for a bathroom break, so let's take some callers and tell me how you feel, Philly. Let's go to our next caller. What's your name, buddy?" Host John Kincade asks.

Detective Lahm pulls into the station's parking lot and parks his car. He's just about to turn off the engine and head inside, but the caller on the radio catches his attention.

"Hello John, first-time caller, long-time listener,
for years the Flyers have kept us a prisoner.
Tonight, I'll spare a life no matter the outcome,
but every playoff loss will result in the death of more than one.
If the Flyers win it all and end up on top,
that's when the killing will forever stop.
If they fail to win Lord Stanley's Cup,
then, next season, the bodies will once again pile up." The alleged "Philly Poet" warns, using a voice disguising application, and abruptly hangs up.

"Okay, then, it looks like we have some more crackpots out there who think they're the next MVD or the 'Philly Poet,'" John Kincade sarcastically says, not believing the caller is the killer.

"That guy sounds really crazy, but the Flyers better not get lazy. Or it's an early exit after the first round and we'll have to wait until next season comes around," MVD says in rapping style as he returns to the radio booth from his bathroom break.

"MVD, you can't take a restroom break while we're on the air anymore. I need you to screen these calls," John Kincade says.

Detective Lahm turns off the car and hurries into the station to report to the captain. He knows that the caller on the radio is the killer by the style of the poem he just read on air, despite the radio host's belief it was just a prank caller.

"I'm telling you, captain, it was him. I'm certain of it. The tone of the poem he read; this could be a huge break for us," he tells the captain after explaining what he just heard on the radio.

"I don't know, Lahm. This city has 1.6 million people, so it was probably a prank caller. However, follow through with it and go down to the radio station to see if you can track the call or if they have anything else to help us. I'll call the radio station manager and let them know you're coming," the captain orders.

"Thanks, Cap. I'll keep you posted if I find out anything. Are you going to tonight's game?" Detective Lahm asks.

"Nah, I'm saving my energy for the playoffs. Tonight's game is meaningless, and the killer has already said he isn't acting on this game's outcome. I'll give my tickets to my son and his wife," the captain replies.

Detective Lahm leaves the captain's office and walks toward the exit. He quickly snags a whole can of Coca-Cola off of Detective Torino's desk while he is down the hall logging in some evidence on a case he's working on.

Game one of the Stanley Cup Playoffs between the Philadelphia Flyers and New York Islanders just finished, and it was a hard-fought contest. The Islanders won 3-2 in overtime. There are extra uniformed and undercover police around the arena looking for anyone suspicious. They all know the killer will be striking tonight because of the loss.

The sports bars around town have undercover police dressed in Flyer's sports clothes and hats, hoping to catch the killer in the act. Detective Lahm is patrolling the streets in his car a few miles around the arena. There are no signs or reports of trouble anywhere, even after a Philly loss.

The post-game press conference with coach Ike Flowers is underway, and the room is packed with nearly ten times more reporters than usual. The reporters are from several countries because the story has gone global.

"Coach Flowers, how are the players holding up knowing they just killed one or more people tonight with that loss?" Reporter one comes out swinging.

"Are you fucking kidding me with that question? Go fuck off and die, you insensitive prick!" Coach Flowers replies, not holding back either.

"Coach, do you feel the 'Philly Poet' could come after you or any of the players if you get eliminated from the playoffs?" Another reporter asks.

"I can't with these fucking questions tonight. I'm too pissed and need to go. I'm outta here!" Coach Flowers shouts as he storms out of the room.

The Flyer's playoff watch party at James Stanwick's house has ended. His friends left disappointed and probably needed to be in better shape to drive from alcohol consumption. James walks the last of his guests, his best friend Mac, to his car.

"You sure you're okay with driving a Mac? You've had a few old fashions," James asks, feeling tipsy.

"I'm good, Jimbo; you make those things weak as fuck. Plus, look at me; I'm a big dude. It takes a lot to get me fucked up," he replies.

"Text me when you get home. Tell Sarah we hope she feels better, and it's her fault they lost because she was not here. Oh, and don't let the 'Philly Poet' get you on the way home!" he laughs.

"Hey, didn't you say Coach Flowers lives in this neighborhood? We should go knock on his door and bitch him out for that performance," Mac suggests.

"You know he's got police protection around his house after tonight; just go home, Mac," James shoots down his dumb idea.

James watches his best friend drive off and goes back into the house. His wife, Kelly, is cleaning the kitchen, and the kids have already gone to bed. James walks into the kitchen and starts helping his wife.

"Hey babe, why don't you clean the living room? I'll finish up here. We can finish up the rest in the morning. I need you to fuck that loss out of me tonight!" She says with a sexy smile.

"Oh, hell yeah!" James replies as he leaves the kitchen to clean the living room.

Kelly is washing up the last of the dishes when she hears a loud crash from the other room. She runs in to see what happened.

"Jim, are you okay? What was that sound? Did something break?" she shouts while entering the living room.

James' body is on the floor after falling through the glass table. He isn't moving, and blood is everywhere. Kelly rushes over to see if he's alive and kneels beside him. James is unconscious but still breathing. His face is slashed open, but she doesn't see any glass shards sticking out of him. Kelly looks at one of the large pieces of broken glass and sees the reflection of a person wearing a black ski mask standing behind her. The intruder strikes at her with a hockey stick, but she quickly moves out of the way. The stick of lumber-turned weapon misses her but strikes James in the throat, cutting him open even more. She runs to the kitchen, and the home invader gives chase.

Kelly grabs a large butcher knife and is ready to go to battle. She stands defiantly behind the kitchen island, and the attacker tries swinging the hockey stick at her from the other side, but it's unable to reach her. She notices the ski mask has a Flyer's logo centered on the forehead area and realizes this could be the "Philly Poet."

The front door opens, and Mac enters.

"Hey Jimbo and Kelly, I forgot my cell phone. If you can hear me, I'm just going to grab it and leave," Mac shouts.

"Mac, Help! In the kitchen, I'm being attacked!" Kelly shouts.

Mac comes running towards the kitchen and sees James' motionless body on the ground, surrounded by broken glass and blood. He continues towards the kitchen.

"What the fuck?" Mac says in disbelief.

The killer turns his attention towards the kitchen entryway, waiting for Mac to come through to take a swing at him. Kelly throws the knife at the killer, and it sticks briefly into his shoulder, just long enough to cause the intruder to drop the hockey stick. Mac enters the kitchen and, without hesitation, grabs the man in a tight bear hug, then body slams him to the ground. The intruder gets up and runs past Mac, escaping the house. Mac gives chase but is much slower than the assailant, so he gets away by running down the street. Mac returns to the house, and Kelly is already on the phone with the 911 operator.

Detective Lahm arrives at the Stanwick home shortly after midnight. Several police cars and countless nosey neighbors are outside.

"Is James the 'Philly Poet'?" one of the neighbors yells at Detective Lahm, who ignores the stupid question.

He enters the house and sees that Dr. Huang is already looking over the now lifeless body of James Stanwick. The second blow to his throat sealed his fate. Detective Lahm thinks to himself, *how the fuck is Dr. Huang always at these crime scenes before him? She must have no life.*

He approaches her, knowing that a silly term of endearment is coming his way once she sees him. He takes a deep breath from the disappointment another person has paid the ultimate price for a Flyer's loss.

"Hey, Dr. Huang, what do we have? I heard the killer was injured, and we have witnesses?" He asks Dr. Huang while she's inspecting the body.

"Oh, hey there, Cherry Lambsickle. Yes, the wife and best friend are being interviewed in the kitchen, and another friend is upstairs with the kids," she reports.

"Are the wounds consistent with our killer?" He asks.

"Yes, Lamb shanks. We finally can confirm my theory that our victims were killed with a hockey stick, which is lying on the kitchen floor," Dr. Huang informs him.

"Great, this might be the break we need. Hopefully, we can get a print off it and find this son-of-a-bitch," Detective Lahm says with optimism.

Detective Lahm enters the kitchen to ask Mac and Kelly some questions and get some details of tonight's tragic event. Kelly is crying on Mac's shoulders, and the uniformed police officer is standing there with his notepad.

"I've got this officer. Why don't you go outside and canvas the neighbors to see if they witnessed anything unusual," Detective Lahm suggests.

"Yes, sir. Here are my notes so far," the officer says while tearing off a piece of paper from his notepad.

"Hello, my name is Detective Kreg 'with a K' Lahm. I'm sorry for your loss. Please tell me any details you can remember of the killer," Detective Lahm says while introducing himself.

Mac and Kelly begin explaining the whole thing in full detail. Detective Lahm is recording the conversation on his cell phone.

Coach Ike "The Enforcer" Flowers is standing next to a reporter just moments before game 7 of the Stanley Cup at the *Wells Fargo Center.*

"Coach, how do you feel about tonight's game? Doesn't get any better than a game 7," the reporter asks.

"Well, it goes without saying. We need to win this fucking game," the coach replies.

The reporter follows up, "You've been favoring that shoulder for a couple weeks now, coach. How did you hurt it?"

"Old age. Flares up when I'm stressed and get asked stupid fucking questions," he colorfully answers.

The game has been a battle, and the Philadelphia Flyers are winning Game 7 of the Stanley Cup finals, 4-2, against the Las Vegas Golden Knights, with only a minute left. Detective Lahm watches the game at his usual sports bar with many patrons and other cops, including Detective Torino Ortez and Dr. Korona Huang. He's excited that this could end the Flyer's Stanley Cup drought and conclude the string of murders by the "Philly Poet." He notices for the first time during the whole game that local sports talk star John Kincade, MVD, and a few others are at a table in the far corner cheering on the Flyers, too. He's a little star-struck for a moment, but that's quickly interrupted by the sound of...

"Score! What a shot! And there's 38 seconds still on the clock. This isn't over yet, folks," the TV announcer says after a slap shot by one of the Golden Knight's defensemen passes through the Flyer's goalie's legs.

The entire bar goes quiet, and nervousness sets in every person watching. They know 38 seconds with an extra attacker can feel like an eternity.

"Come on Flyers, don't fucking blow this game. We need this!" one of the sports bar customers yells, breaking the silence.

This inspires the patrons of the entire bar to start chanting, "Let's go, Flyers!" repeatedly. Detective Lahm closes his eyes and thinks of the 19 victims during the regular season and the 6 victims during the playoffs. Strangely, he wants the Flyers to win so their deaths aren't entirely in vain, and of course, the killing will stop. He decides to leave his eyes closed for the rest of the game.

"The Knights are giving it their all with the extra attacker. Philly is having trouble clearing the puck with 10 seconds left!" The TV announcer reports.

The tension in the bar is thicker than a Philly cheesesteak from *Pat's King of Steaks* in South Philadelphia.

"He shoots! What a save, and Hobelchek clears the puck with 5 seconds left," the TV announcer continues his play-by-play.

"5, 4, 3, 2, 1!" the entire bar counts down to victory.

Everyone jumps up and starts hugging and high-fiving each other. Dr. Huang grabs Detective Lahm and kisses him.

"They did it, Lambchop! They won!" she says after laying a nice wet smacker on his lips.

Detective Kreg "with a K" Lahm doesn't mind it. He can't believe what happened, so he grabs Detective Torino's beer and slams it.

"Lahm, that's my beer man. Wait a minute, are you the one that keeps stealing food and drinks off my desk for the past five fucking years?" He realizes.

"Wow, some great detective work there, Torino," Dr. Huang says.

"Fuck it, I don't care. The Flyers won!" Detective Torino says as everyone laughs and continues to celebrate the victory.

"Man, the captain must be having a blast at the game. There's nothing better in sports than a game 7 Stanley Cup final," Detective Lahm claims.

The whole bar is jumping with happiness. Detective Lahm decides to go to John Kincade's table to meet and congratulate them.

"Hey, Mr. Kincade and MVD, I'm Detective Kreg 'with a K' Lahm, and I'm a big fan of your show. I just wanted to come over and say hello and thank you for all the morning entertainment you provide. And GO FLYERS!" Detective Lahm says.

"Damn, glad to meet you, detective. Let me buy you a beer for the victory and all you do for the city," John Kincade responds.

"Hold on right there, I'll get this round; I'm wondering, detective, if the killer will ever be found. Now that the Flyers have finally won, do you think the killing will be done?" MVD says in his locally famous rhyming style.

Wow, he actually still rhymes off the air, too, Detective Lahm thinks.

After listening to him on the radio for years and during the investigation, he recognizes a familiar tone to his rhymes. He gives MVD a suspicious look.

"I sure hope he's done killing. In one of his poems, he said he would be, but we'll still find him. What do you think?" Detective Lahm asks, curious about his response.

"*I think he's probably a very happy man, unless, of course, he's also a 76ers fan*," MVD replies with a sinister smile as he walks away from the bar to retrieve a round of drinks.

The End?
76ers last championship was 1983, over 40 years ago.

ROLL TIDE!

"Blake Powers takes a knee to end the game, and the number one-seeded Michigan Wolverines have defeated #4 seed Alabama in the college football semi-final playoffs. They'll play the winner of tonight's Ohio State/LSU game for the national championship next week, right here on CBS," says the network and game's play-by-play announcer, Bernie Jordan, to the millions watching.

"This could be a re-match of their epic battle a month ago in Columbus, where the Wolverines won 41-40 on a last-second field goal. At that time, Ohio State was ranked #1, and Michigan #4. Both schools were undefeated. The USC loss to Utah allowed Ohio State to only drop to #3, keeping them in the college playoffs," CBS color commentator and former NFL legend Marcus Danby adds.

"Alabama returned to the top 4 after their first loss against LSU a few weeks back because LSU crushed Georgia in the SEC championship game to knock the Bulldogs out of the top 4," Bernie explains.

"The Buckeyes defeated Alabama last year in the national championship game and will have a chance to repeat if they beat LSU tonight. Michigan can win their first championship since 1997. Whoever wins, it will be one for the ages," Marcus promotes the possible upcoming outcomes.

The college football playoff game between the University of Michigan and the University of Alabama that just concluded was the Cotton Bowl, played in Dallas, Texas, at the *AT&T Stadium* on New Year's Eve. The Michigan fans in attendance are still excited, while the Alabama faithful are exiting with their heads hanging low.

Alabama is expected to win the national championship yearly, and this season will be considered a failure. Losing two years in a row to a Big 10 team in the college playoffs is unacceptable because in Alabama... It goes from God to football to the rest of the world.

Mark Stockton is standing in the Cotton Bowl crowd, high-fiving his fellow Wolverine fans. He graduated from Michigan two years ago and relocated to Dallas for work two months ago. Mark attended the game by himself. Being new to the city and working most of the week, he has little time for a social life. Mark got to know a group of Wolverine fans sitting in his section that traveled from Michigan for the game. They invited him to join them tonight at a local bar to bring in the new year and celebrate the Wolverine victory.

A couple of intoxicated Alabama fans walking up the stairs towards the exit didn't appreciate Mark and his new friends' excessive high-fiving and excitement. One of the drunk men threw his shoulder into Mark as he passed by, causing Mark to fall into his seat. The group started yelling at the two men as they continued their stair climb of defeat. Mark got up and ran after them.

"Hey bro, what's up? You don't have to be a sore loser and douchebag!" Mark shouts at the man as he aggressively taps him on the shoulder.

The man stops climbing the steps and turns around. Mark didn't truly realize the size of the drunken fan and quickly regretted his decision to confront this giant. He's easily over 6 feet tall and about 300 lbs. with a religious cross tattooed on the right side of his neck and the Alabama "A" on his left side. Mark briefly thought this could be one of the Crimson Tide offensive linemen.

He notices the man starting to clench his fist and raise it to strike him down. The beast of a man was also a step higher than Mark, giving him the high-ground advantage—not that he needed it. Mark braces for impact, but it never comes. Instead, the man smiles, turns around, and continues his climb, eventually getting mixed into the departing sea of crimson and white.

Mark turns around to return to his seating area and discovers why the man decided not to pummel him. A large group of Michigan fans are standing right behind him for protection. This made him feel safe and proud to be a Michigan fan. He nearly got "emotional" from the act of camaraderie by the Wolverine nation.

"I can't believe you stood up to that huge guy. You're really brave," one of the female Michigan fans flirts.

"Yeah, I couldn't just let him get away with knocking me over and not saying anything to him," he replies with a sense of toughness.

"I'm glad you agreed to come out with us tonight. It will be a great time, and you owe me a dance," she says.

"I do? I don't recall you asking for a dance?" He replies.

"I didn't. You owe me one for backing you up and ensuring your face didn't become a part of the concrete stairs. I'm Julie, by the way," she says with a humorous, flirtatious smile.

"Fair enough. I'm Mark. It's nice to meet you, Julie," he responds with a blushing face.

"It's over; The Ohio State Buckeyes have defeated LSU in a blowout, 38-10. They were clearly on a mission today," ABC network Sportscaster Brian Galloway announces the Fiesta Bowl game when the clock reaches 0:00.

"Perhaps Michigan's win earlier today gave them that extra spark they needed to dominate this game," Color commentator Shelly Marquez suggests.

"The two Big 10 Juggernauts will battle once again next week. This time, it's in Miami at the Orange Bowl. Ohio State will seek revenge for their one-point loss last month to the Wolverines and repeat as national champs. Michigan will be searching for their first championship since 1997," Brian points out what is at stake for both schools.

The Fiesta Bowl in Phoenix, Arizona, concludes with Ohio State University defeating Louisiana State University and earning their way to the national championship. One fact about a blowout in any football game, college or pro, is that most of the losing team's fans have left by the end. This allows the winning team's fanbase to congregate in the stands and move closer to the field.

Kevin Staley is one of those fans who left his purchased seat and advanced several rows closer into the now-emptied seat once occupied by a hopeful LSU fan. The Buckeye fans are going wild and have surrounded an older couple who are the only LSU fans in the section. The older man is wearing an LSU jersey, and his wife is wearing an Alabama T-shirt. However, she supported LSU during the game for her husband and stayed faithful to the SEC conference.

"Why don't you fuckin' leave with the rest of your redneck fans?" a man shouts in the face of the older couple.

"Hey everyone, easy on the old-timers. You're in Buckeye country now; I'm sure it's past your bedtime. Perhaps you should leave now to make it home in time for the next Antiques Roadshow episode," Kevin says while high-fiving the other OSU fans around him.

"Unlike you, I've paid for these seats. Therefore, my wife and I will stay to see every minute of the game," the old man replies.

"Well, I can respect that Grandpa. However, as you probably can't see the scoreboard without your glasses, the game is over now. These fans are getting rowdy, so please depart this area for your safety. The Big Ten rules college football now, not the Suck-E-C." Kevin says while pointing to the exit.

The old couple doesn't say another word, gets out of their seats, and pushes their way through the cluster of red and white until they reach the stairs that lead them out. The old man gives Kevin one last long stare, making him uneasy.

The group of OSU fans chants, "Na na na, na na na, hey hey hey, good-bye!" multiple times until the old couple is no longer in sight.

Kevin moved to the Phoenix area a few years ago with a couple of college buddies from Ohio State University. They're also in attendance but mixed in somewhere among the ocean of Buckeye faithful. They'll meet in the parking lot outside *State Farm Stadium*. In the meantime, Kevin is having a blast celebrating with other OSU fans standing next to him.

The bar is packed with people preparing for the new year to arrive. The sounds of great dance music, the buzz of a thousand conversations, and the shuffling of feet on the dance floor fill the air. Mark is dancing with Julie, and she's grinding on his leg. He's feeling the best he has since moving to Dallas. The other Michigan fans are slamming shots at the table and singing the Michigan fight song, "The Victors," causing Mark to produce the biggest smile.

"What are you so happy about?" Julie shouts.

"Because it's been a great fucking day!" Mark shouts back as he pulls her into him and kisses her.

After dancing, they return to the table and slam the two shots of *Patron* tequila waiting there for them, and more high-fives are distributed throughout the group.

"Hey, is anybody here interested in getting tickets to the Orange Bowl and going to watch Michigan become national champs?" Mark asks the group.

"Hell no, we can't afford that shit. We could barely afford this trip," one of the Michigan fans responds as if he is speaking for the entire group.

"Sorry, sweetie, I can't make that one," Julie replies disappointedly.

"Fuck it, I'll go alone. Go Blue!" Mark yells out, and the group returns with a loud "Go Blue!".

Kevin finds his two buddies walking back to the car in the stadium parking lot. He catches up to them, and they all start yelling and high-fiving.

"What a fucking game? We're going to kick Michigan's ass!" One of his friends shouts out.

"Hell yeah. Who wants to go to the game in Miami? I'll get tickets tomorrow," Kevin asks his friends.

"I can't. I have to work. There's no way they'll give me the time off," one of the friends replies.

"Yeah, sorry, man. I can't afford to take the time off work; I need the money for rent," the other friend adds.

"Fuck man, this means I have to go alone? You guys suck," he returns, agitated by his friends' lack of commitment to OSU.

They continue their celebratory walk to the car, weaving through the line of cars, trying to leave the parking lot, and giving high-fives to any OSU fan they pass.

The college football national championship, held in Miami, Florida, at the *Hard Rock Stadium*, is only a few days away. The remaining tickets sold out minutes after Michigan and Ohio State victories. Every sports fan knows this will be the most watched and historic championship game ever. The city of Miami and *Hard Rock Stadium* have been preparing for this game for a few weeks.

However, late-breaking news reports that an unseasonal hurricane is changing directions and heading toward Miami. It is expected to make landfall on Friday, only three days before the national championship game. Hurricane Matthew has already reached category 5 and is expected to cause massive amounts of damage and flooding. The NCAA is currently debating whether to push back the national championship or move it to another location on a last-minute's notice.

Mark is home in his Dallas apartment, watching Sportscenter as they report on Hurricane Matthew approaching Miami.

"This will be the first hurricane to hit Florida in January. The unseasonable warm weather in the Caribbean has created this monster of a storm that has already reached category 5 status. Experts are preparing for major damage to the city and coastlines. Evacuations and preparations are already underway in Miami." ESPN correspondent John Raymond reports from outside the *Hard Rock Stadium* in Miami.

"John, do you think the NCAA will move or postpone the title game between Michigan and Ohio State?" Scott Van Pelt asks from the Sportscenter studio.

"Good Question, Scott; at this point, they will most likely relocate the game to play on Monday. The possible damage is too risky. They have ruled out New Orleans because of the Saints playoff game on Sunday and *AT&T Stadium* in Dallas because of a Monster Truck show this weekend. Hurricane Matthew's path has also eliminated Atlanta as a possible site. Sources tell me it appears to be *Bryant-Denny Stadium* at the University of Alabama," he replies.

"Obviously, this would be historic and remain on a neutral site for the teams. I wouldn't anticipate too many Bama fans attending that game, with Ohio State and Michigan beating them in the past two years and eliminating them from winning another national championship," Scott Van Pelt jokes.

"The NCAA is going to allow fans who have bought tickets to the game in Miami the first opportunity to exchange them for tickets in Tuscaloosa or refund them before selling other tickets. This process will begin today at 1 p.m. Eastern time. Ticket holders can go online and choose their seats based on price. *Bryant-Denny Stadium* has about 30,000 more seats than *Hard Rock Stadium*, so more tickets can be sold," John adds.

"I'm sure this will cause major travel changes for fans planning to attend. How does the NCAA plan to deal with that?" Scott Van Pelt asks.

"The NCAA has contacted the airlines and hotels to help accommodate the traveling fans. The NCAA can be criticized for many things, but they seem to be on the ball with this situation," John answers.

"Thank you, John; we just all pray for the safety of Miami and Florida residents affected by Hurricane Matthew," Scott Van Pelt states.

Mark turns off the T.V. and is upset about the news. He texts Julie, who is now back in Michigan, about the news.

I can't fucking believe this. The game could be played here in Dallas, but a redneck monster truck rally instead? I don't want to go to Alabama.

She texts back a minute later.

You should still go; I'm sure it will be fun. Just don't fall in love with some hick.

Mark sends a *LOL* reply and returns to his work computer. He'll wait until 1 p.m. Eastern time to exchange his ticket, change his flight, and find a hotel.

Kevin and his friend are at a local sports bar in Tempe, Arizona. They're watching the news report about Hurricane Matthew's destructive path closing in on Miami, Florida.

"This fucking hurricane is going to screw up my chance to meet hot Miami Latina chicks and see the Buckeyes win the national championship against the Michigan marmots," Kevin says as he slams his fist down on the bar causing a rattling sound from plates and utensils.

"Hey, easy over there, Kev!" The barkeep warns.

"Sorry Big Tim! My bad. I'm just pissed about this hurricane fucking up my plans to go to Miami for the game," he tries to rationalize his moment of anger.

"Bro, just go to the game in Alabama. You get the first crack at tickets since you have already bought one. Plus, you didn't book your flight yet, so it's no problem," his friend suggests.

"Man, there are no chicks in Alabama. And if there is one, she's probably missing her teeth or drinking Miller Lite," he answers.

"Kev, you're looking at this the wrong way. First, any OSU female fans at the game will be from somewhere other than Alabama, thus increasing the odds of hotness. Second, no Alabama fan will be at that game. They hate all of the Big 10, especially Michigan and OSU. I would say your chances of hooking up are arguably better," Big Tim replies with the extraordinary wisdom that any great barkeep should possess.

"That's a great point. I guess I'm going to Alabama this weekend. Do they have airports there?" Kevin says with a snicker as he pulls out his phone from his pocket to book the trip.

Kevin sits in his aisle seat on his Southwest flight that departed Phoenix and is heading to Birmingham, Alabama. The flight is on a layover at the Dallas/Fort Worth airport, and all passengers who had Dallas as their scheduled destination have departed the plane. The Southwest agents have started boarding the awaiting Dallas passengers heading to Birmingham. Kevin does what most men would do: People watch every boarding passenger in hopes that the hottest woman sits in the empty middle seat next to him.

A potential candidate approaches, and she looks directly at Kevin. She pauses, staring at the empty middle chair, starts putting her small luggage overhead, and begins to stake her claim to row 11, Seat B. She's gorgeous, and Kevin gives her the biggest smile as he stands up to let her pass to the middle seat. The woman looks over at the passenger sitting in the window seat in the same row. He's a large man who appears to be dirty with stained clothes. He's asleep and snoring, with parts of his fat leaking into the middle chair area. She glances down the airplane's middle and sees an empty seat three more rows back. She pulls back her luggage and takes the better seating option in row 14.

"Fuck. I should move seats after we landed. This fat fuck is going to scare away all the women," he mutters to himself as he sits back down.

"Please take the first seat you see, as we will have a full flight. The seats from rows 12 to the back are full," the flight attendant instructs and informs.

An older businessman approaches Kevin's aisle but suddenly stops and takes the middle seat, Row 10, Seat E. The next passenger, right behind the businessman, is a young man about the same age as Kevin. Since it's the last open seat, it belongs to this guy. The young man approaches row 11, noticing each other's baseball caps and hoodies... Row 11, Seat C team OSU vs Row 11, Seat B team U of M. Game on.

Kevin doesn't get up to allow the young man to pass, making the journey to his seat more challenging for the Wolverine fan as he tries to squeeze through to the middle seat.

"Bro, you couldn't get up?" he says to Kevin.

"Sorry, man, but Buckeye Nation will always make things difficult for Michigan. You're fine, and good luck with that seat," Kevin replies.

The young man sits down and tries not to touch the bare skin of the large gut spilling into his chair. Kevin looks over and laughs to himself.

"Hi, I'm Mark. Are you going to the game too? Sucks they had to move it to Alabama," Mark introduces himself with an attempt at small talk.

"Look, man, I don't want to talk to you on this flight or anywhere else. Being a Michigan fan, you've already increased the chances of this plane going down," Kevin replies.

"And how does my presence increase the chances of this plane crashing?" he asks, laughing at the silly comment.

"Because God doesn't want Michigan fans that close to Heaven," Kevin answers, laughing at his *perfectly* crafted joke.

Mark chuckles, thinking that was a good one, but he focuses on his phone. He realizes the OSU superfan beside him won't be pleasant to speak with, and he doesn't want to wake up "Sleeping Beastly" next to him for conversation.

Mark's struggling not to vomit with the odor that is next to him. He's spent the first hour of the flight with his nose and mouth tucked away into his shirt.

"I can't take this much more. Bro, wash up in the bathroom and get rid of that B.O. you got," Mark says to Kevin.

"What? That stench isn't me. It's the big man next to you," Kevin defends himself.

"Oh, I assumed it was you since it smells like the Ohio State campus," Mark quips back, equally proud of his set-up joke.

"Oh ha ha, real fucking funny. You know we'll both probably smell like fatty after this flight. I already can't wait to take a shower. That reminds me, what's the best way to kill a Michigan fan? You slam the toilet lid while he's drinking water," Kevin jokes.

"Nice one. How many OSU freshmen does it take to screw in a light bulb? Zero, it's a sophomore-level course," Mark returns fire.

The flight arrived on time, and the weather in Birmingham, Alabama, was chilly with light rain. Mark and Kevin are excited to escape the giant odor ball beside them. They gather their carry-on bags and walk the single file line off the airplane. Kevin says "thank you and goodbye" to the cute flight attendant standing at the front of the plane, saying her farewells to the passengers. Mark, walking behind Kevin, notices the flight attendant turn her head in disgust at the horrible body odor now latched onto them. Mark catches up to Kevin in the jetway.

"Damn, bro, you're right. We stink! That flight attendant nearly gagged as we passed by," Mark tells Kevin.

"Nah, that's not the smell. It's just how most women react to Wolverine fans," Kevin replies.

"Jokes aside, do you want to split an Uber to the University of Alabama? It's an hour away and could be pricy. Don't worry; I won't talk to you in the car," Mark asks.

"Yeah, fuck it. Why not?" Kevin answers.

They exit the jetway and enter the arrival gate. The two rival fans briefly stop to look for the sign pointing them toward "Ride Share" or "Exit." The cute woman from row 14 passes by both of them.

"Jesus, what fucking died? It smells like Ann Arbor, Michigan, and Columbus, Ohio, had a baby together in the back of a Greyhound bus. Go shower, for all of our sake. Roll Tide!" She says to them.

The two men are standing outside the airport, waiting for their Uber driver to arrive. One is decked out in scarlet and grey; the other sports his maize and blue team colors. They're both excited to get to their hotel, get cleaned up, and enjoy a night out around campus on a Saturday night—separately, of course!

"I can't believe we're staying at the same hotel. I thought OSU fans only sleep in halfway houses," Mark jokes.

"Funny. Look, don't go to the same bars I'm going to. I want to get laid tonight, and you'll scare all the fish away," Kevin replies.

"Don't worry, I don't go to gay bars," Mark responds.

The Uber car arrived, and the two "enemies" put their bags in the trunk and got into the vehicle. The interior of the Ford Focus is decked out with Crimson Tide décor everywhere. The seats are Crimson Red with a white A embroidered on them. There's a Nick Saban bobblehead on the dashboard, and the driver is wearing a University of Alabama T-shirt and hat.

"Great, we have Bama' superfan driving us. Does he know that they lost last week to your shitty team, with the refs helping them?" Kevin whispers to Mark.

"He's probably an Ohio State alumnus since he drives an Uber for a living," Mark jokes.

The driver starts driving away once the men are securely buckled in and the doors are closed. He doesn't say a word to greet them or make any small talk. Mark and Kevin just assume that he's all business.

For the first fifteen minutes, the car's only voices come from the sports talk radio program the driver is listening to. They're discussing the only sports-related topic in Alabama... Crimson Tide football. Kevin's reading about the upcoming game on the ESPN app, and Mark is playing Candy Crush.

"Hey bro, do these guys on the radio know that Alabama's season is over, or do they talk about Alabama football all year?" Kevin decides to start the conversation with a snarky comment to the driver.

"Leave him alone; I'm sure they have a basketball team, too. Although, you never hear about them," Mark jumps in.

"Bama football is #1 in these parts, and you'll want to remember that while you're here. Roll Tide!" the driver warns.

"Except you have the two teams that ruined Bama's chances the last two years at a national championship playing in their own stadium. That's like a Big Ten slap in the face," Kevin responds.

"Fixed! Everybody knows that the NCAA told the referees to ensure that Bama lost so we wouldn't dominate college football yearly. We'll be back next year. Roll Tide!" the driver passionately explains the losses.

"I don't know, man; I think it's time for Saban to retire or get fired," Kevin says, trying to get under the driver's skin.

The driver pulls the car over at a nearby gas station before entering the I-20 highway to Tuscaloosa, home of the Crimson Tide.

"You stinky motherfuckers need to get out of my car right now. You don't bad mouth, Mr. Saban. You can walk the rest of the way. Most of us Uber drivers are on a group chat, and I'll put the word out to decline your request for a ride. You should start walking now. Roll Tide!" the driver commands.

"Are you fucking joking right now? You can't kick us out. You'll take us to our hotel, and you can do nothing about it!" Kevin responds.

The driver pulls out his Sig Sauer P365 handgun, turns towards the Big Ten fans, and points the weapon at them. Kevin and Mark immediately jump out of the vehicle. The driver speeds off, leaving them stranded at the Chevron station.

"Hey, wait, our fucking bags!" Mark yells out.

The driver sticks his hand out the window, gives them the middle finger, and says one last loud... "Roll Tide!"

"Fuck. I left my wallet in my bag. I'll call Uber and make him bring our shit back," Kevin says.

An hour later, they're still sitting on a bench outside the Chevron gas station, where they were abandoned.

"I don't think he's coming back. Either Uber didn't give him the message, or he ignored it." Mark states.

"They're all in on it. You heard the driver; they have a group chat, and whatever redneck fuck that runs the Alabama Uber is in on it too. We have to find a cab," Kevin replies.

"And I guess I'm paying for it since your wallet is on its way to the trailer park shack the driver lives in?" Mark asks.

The store owner and one of the clerks exit the store and approach the bench. Mark nudges Kevin to alert him of their presence.

"You bums need to leave the area. There's no loitering around my store," the owner commands.

"Bums? He must be referring to you since you have that Michigan gear on," Kevin says, laughing at his joke.

"Relax, sir. I'll come in and buy a couple of Cokes and hot dogs. We're just waiting for our ride," Mark offers.

"You need to leave now. You're not going into my store; we don't serve your kind here," the owner says.

"Wow, because he's black? That's fucking racist." Kevin says with an angry tone while pointing at Mark.

"No dumb shit. What do you think this is, 1952? It's because of the school colors you're wearing. Get your Yankee asses out of here now. Roll Tide!" The owner commands.

The two rival fans get up and start walking. To where? They have no idea. Kevin continues trying to order another Uber or Lyft driver, but he keeps getting declined by the drivers. He looks up the closest car rental place to their location while Mark continues to call cab companies.

"Fuck, these cab places are telling me they don't have cabs available all day, or they won't answer my call," he tells Kevin.

"That's okay. There's an Enterprise Car Rental place about 3 miles from here. They close in 2 hours, so we'll follow Pike Rd and rent a car. I'll reimburse you half of the amount when I get my debit card back. I can still use Apple Pay where it's available, but I'll need to cancel all my cards soon," Kevin suggests.

"That sounds good. I can't believe how tight the Uber and Lyft drivers are here. It's quite impressive. If the Buckeye football team were half that connected, then they'd have a chance at beating Michigan," Mark replies.

They begin their long 3-mile walk to get transportation and give up on trying to secure a ride-share vehicle. The rivals don't say much to each other besides and occasionally jab at the other's team or fanbase. The road hardly has any traffic in either direction. Mark and Kevin thought about hitch-hiking but figured nobody around here would pick up two guys wearing Michigan and Ohio State hoodies, t-shirts, and hats. Kevin even has OSU Nike shoes on.

A crimson-red pickup truck comes driving up from behind them. Two people are in the front, and three more guys are sitting in the truck bed. They both turn around to see what is approaching them from the rear, and Kevin is struck in the forehead with a half-full Miller Lite beer can, followed by a loud "Roll Tide!" chant.

"Oh shit! They know what Ohio State fan's favorite beer is," Mark says as Kevin falls back from the beer can blow.

The truck passes them and pulls off to the side of the road several feet ahead. The five men quickly exit the truck and run towards the two out-of-towners. Mark helps Kevin get up, and they begin running away from the Alabama faithful. Kevin notices a Birmingham police car approaching the upcoming intersection. He starts waving frantically for their attention. The police officer turns and drives towards them. The cop sees five local boys chasing the two out-of-towners and continues driving past them.

"Are you fucking kidding me? He just kept going," Kevin complains.

"Yeah, he sees what's happening and turns a blind eye. One of these redneck fucks is probably both his son and uncle," Mark replies.

The men catch up to the "Big 10" guys and surround them. They examine the group to decide which will be the toughest to fight. Mark sets his travel bag down and puts up his guard. Kevin stands back-to-back with him and prepares his fists. The group of men starts laughing at their attempt to fight.

"Well, well, well. Look what we got here, Jim Bob," one of the Bama men says.

Mark looks over at the man who spoke and recognizes him. He's one of the behemoth Alabama fans from the game last week who was going to fight.

"I'll be damned, Cletus, if it isn't our buddy from Dallas?" Jim Bob replies.

"Are their names really Cletus and Jim Bob? That figures," Kevin asks sarcastically.

"Doesn't look like you have a whole lotta people this time backing you up besides this Ohio State shithead," Cletus observes.

"Friends of yours, Blue? Look, fellas, I've got no beef here; you know I hate Michigan more than you do. So, I'll just keep walking, and you can hang out with your Michigan buddy here," Kevin says, trying to weasel his way out of the situation.

"Well, see, here's the problem. Hey Sawyer, show him your tat!" Cletus responds to Kevin's request.

Sawyer, a smaller guy with a rugged look, removes his shirt and reveals a tattoo that says *2024 National Champs* (with the Alabama "A" underneath it). That was the previous year when OSU defeated them for the championship.

"Well, that was stupid, but I love your confidence," Kevin responds.

"He got a pretty mouth on him," says a menacing-looking man from the circle of rednecks.

"Oh hell, Rufus likes him. You're in trouble now, boys," Sawyer quips.

"Okay, we have a Rufus, a Sawyer, a Cletus, and a Jim Bob! So, is your name Buck?" Kevin says with more sarcasm to the last of the five men.

"Yeah, it is. Do I know you?" Buck replies.

"Jesus, you can't make this shit up," Kevin says, shaking his head in disbelief.

The five men close in on Kevin and Mark, and the melee ensues. The two Big 10'ers put up a good fight getting a few blows in and knocking Sawyer out, but they were quickly on the ground getting kicked repeatedly by the remaining four rednecks.

Suddenly, out of nowhere, a black Chevrolet Malibu runs over Sawyer's unconscious body and strikes Jim Bob, sending his body huddling several feet in the air. He lands on his head, snapping his neck instantly. Mark and Kevin look up and see a female yelling out of the Malibu's driver-side window, "Get in the fucking car!".

They jump into the vehicle without thinking or caring about who these two saviors are. The car peels off and nearly runs over Cletus. Mark sees the remaining three men jump into the pickup truck and give chase.

"Oh shit, they're coming after us. I guarantee those hicks have a gun in the fucking truck!" Mark yells.

"Hey guys, thank you so much for saving us back there. Who are you, and why did you do it?" Kevin asks.

"We just can't let those Alabama fuckheads ruin our good state of Alabama, can we sweet pickle cock?" The woman replies, looking at her husband driving the car.

"No sugar snatch, we cannot! We're part of a secret group of Auburn Tiger fans who patrol the state and protect people from Bama fanatics. We will get you to safety in Tuscaloosa," the man explains.

"So, you're saying the safest place from Bama's fanatics is at the University of Alabama?" Mark asks.

"You'll be among the OSU and Michigan fans that made it safely. The University doesn't want negative press with fans getting hurt, so it's the safest place. But first, we need to lose these psycho hillbillies," The man answers.

"Turn right up here, my super sausage," The woman orders.

The man makes a sharp right turn, and the guys crash into each other in the back seat. They quickly realize they're not buckled in and do so. The red pickup takes the turn a bit slower, and they get further away from them. The man notices something ahead blocking the road.

"Candy Clit, what is that up ahead in the road?" he asks.

"You two got some interesting terms of endearment for each other. It's kind of cute," Kevin says.

"Dude, you trying to join their upside-down pineapple club or something? Fucking an OSU fan is worse than getting gonorrhea," Mark adds.

"You would know," Kevin responds.

Then suddenly, the man's head explodes from a bullet coming through the front windshield and splatters all over Kevin's face. The car swerves, but the woman grabs the steering wheel and straightens the car out. The man's foot pushes down on the gas uncontrollably from his dead body.

"Oh my God, no! You shot my Prickly Pear Pecker, you son-of-a-bitch!" She screams, keeping the car headed straight for the now recognizable police car in the middle of the road.

The policeman is on the other side with his elbows resting on the hood and holding an AR-15 tactical assault rifle. He is steadily aiming it at the car. Another shot exits the weapon and pierces through the woman, nearly striking Mark—her blood showers on Kevin's face.

"Great, now I have Bonnie and Clyde's guts all over me. Why the fuck isn't any of this blood getting on you?" Kevin complains.

"Even bullets recognize a giant tampon when they see it," Mark jokes.

They both quickly duck down and close their eyes, hoping for the best as the woman continues to speed towards the police car and screaming, "Die Tide"!

Another shot rings through the air and finds its way through the woman's neck. She slumps over, causing the car to veer off the road, flip onto its top, and crash into a tree. Mark and Kevin are shaken up and suspended upside down from their seat belts. They both press the release button and drop to the ceiling of the car's interior. Mark notices a pair of policeman legs approaching the vehicle.

"Come on out of there and make this easy on yourselves. I'll give you a painless death, unlike my boy Jim Bob had back there when these two Auburnites ran him over," he says while shooting another round into the woman's dead body, startling Mark and Kevin.

"Fuck, I called it. I knew one of those bumpkins was his son." Mark brags.

The policeman gets a few feet away from the car and stops. Kevin notices the glove box is open and sees a pistol. He reaches past the bloody dead woman and grabs it.

"I'll countdown from 5. After that, I'm going to unload on this car. Five... Four... Three..." the cop commands and starts his countdown.

Bang! Bang! Bang!

Three shots come from the car, and one of the bullets hits the policeman in the knee; the other two miss him entirely. However, luckily, one of the stray bullets penetrates Buck's face, who is driving the fast-approaching red pickup truck. The vehicle goes out of control and swerves into the policeman's path. He's unable to move due to his blown-out kneecap. The truck smashed into him at 56MPH and doused Kevin with more blood coming through the smashed passenger window.

The truck crashes into the parked patrol car, sending Cletus through the windshield. Standing in the truck bed like a character from Mad Max, Rufus flies through the air. Mark watches him soar past like he is in slow motion, notices a big smile on his face, and yells his last words, "Roll Tide!" before his body crashes into a large American Elm tree and splits his head wide open.

They crawl out of the smashed car windows and stand up to assess the carnage; everyone's dead, and they feel relieved and terrified at the same time.

"I think I'm gonna puke," Mark says as he runs over to a nearby bush and starts vomiting.

"Let it out, man. Puking because you're scared is nothing to be ashamed of. Michigan football does it every time before they play OSU," Kevin jokes.

"Nah, I thought I just saw an Ohio State sorority girl," Mark replies.

Mark finishes his barf session and notices the amount of blood splattered across Kevin's face.

"Damn, bro, your face looks like an OSU cheerleader's panties... Always bloody," Mark returns fire.

"Look, we need to take the police car since it's the only one that looks like it might still run and get on the road as far as we can," Kevin suggests.

"I think we'll stand out—two guys driving a smashed police car while wearing OSU and Michigan gear. However, we can't walk, and these two other vehicles aren't going anywhere," Mark says.

"We'll need to find some new clothes as soon as possible. The Alabama clothes on these dead rednecks are all torn up and bloody, so we can't blend in." Kevin says.

They walk over to the police car with the keys in the ignition. Kevin gets behind the wheel and tries several times to start the vehicle.

"What's taking so long, bro?" Mark asks.

"It's not starting. You're from Detroit; hot wire it." Kevin commands.

"What? Because I'm black?" Mark asks to embarrass him by pulling the race card.

"Exactly, it's a birthright. That's also why you're not driving; we don't want to get pulled over." Kevin returns with more stereotype jokes.

The next twist of the keys starts the engine. They give each other a quick hi-five, and Kevin drives away from the crash site.

After about 30 minutes of traveling west on the Interstate 20 highway, they began to feel more relaxed. Hardly anybody noticed the police car's damaged right side because Kevin stayed in the right lane to shield it from the view of other drivers passing to the left. However, that didn't stop several odd glances from passengers of other vehicles noticing the two men didn't look like cops driving a police cruiser.

Mark looks in the passenger's side mirror and notices an older white Chevrolet Blazer quickly approaching them with ramming speed.

"Fuck bro, we've been spotted. There must be more country cousins, and they're about to hit us; go faster! Oh, I forgot Ohio State only has one speed. Fucking slow!" Mark says.

"It's about to be *Deliverance*, and you have jokes? I'll tell you this right now, I'm not the one that's going to be squealing like a pig if these hicks catch us," Kevin replies while pressing his foot down on the gas to speed up.

Over the police scanner in the car, the guys heard the report: *"Attention, all cars, we have a stolen police vehicle #524, last seen in Birmingham. Roadblocks have been set up along highways and other streets leading out of the city. Air support will be up soon. These men are considered armed and dangerous."*

"We're not fucking armed or dangerous. How the fuck did we get into this mess?" Kevin complains.

"Fucking Hurricane Matthew, that's how. We should be in Miami with hot women. Instead, Buford and his inbred cousins are chasing us," Mark answers.

"Maybe we've already passed the roadblocks. We just have to get to Tuscaloosa, ditch this car, and blend in with the thousands of OSU fans and a couple hundred Michigan fans," Kevin hopes.

After several more minutes of speeding, weaving around vehicles, and being chased by the white Blazer, Mark notices numerous brake lights ahead of them.

"Fuck! I think there's a roadblock ahead. Those cars are stopping. We can't get caught in this car. Turn off at this exit coming up." Mark suggests.

"Hell no! There's nothing out here. I thought black people were smarter than white people in horror movie situations. *Wrong Turn, Texas Chainsaw Massacre, Duel, The Hills Have Eyes, Children of the Corn, The Hitcher...*" Kevin rambles on before being cut off by Mark.

"Okay, I get it. You were a film major; That doesn't surprise me attending Ohio State. Just make the turn so we don't go to jail or worse. They'll shoot us." Mark commands.

"Fine. I'll turn. But let's be honest. The cops will most likely shoot you, not me." Kevin says while veering off the highway on the exit ramp.

"Exactly why I need you to turn," Mark says.

The white Blazer exits with them, traveling down a two-lane road without traffic. The country homes are acres apart. The Blazer is on the car's back bumper, nearly touching it.

"Where the fuck are we? These farmhouses remind me of that crazy Elkins family in Texas that killed people in the 70s. We have to ditch these mother fuckers and this car," Kevin says with panic in his voice.

"Literally mother fuckers. Do you hear that? Sounds like dueling banjos," Mark jokes.

Kevin doesn't laugh at Mark's *Deliverance* reference as he tries to concentrate on the road and the chasing yokels. Mark starts looking around the car for weapons. He finds a can of pepper spray, a 26" Smith & Wesson baton, and a stun gun. However, his most significant find is the tactical shotgun in a holder between the two front seats until he discovers it is locked. Mark guessed that *Barney Fife*, flattened by the truck, still had the keys to the gun lock on his person.

"After we lose these fried green tomato-eating fucks, we have to ditch this cop car. We'll have to find another way to the game," Mark states.

The white Blazer suddenly clips the rear right bumper of the police car and causes the vehicle to veer off-road and into a ditch. The airbags deploy and smash into the out-of-towner's faces.

"Bro, you okay?" Mark asks.

"Yeah, that felt like an Ohio State linebacker crushing one of Michigan's running backs for a 3-yard loss," Kevin replies.

The white Blazer quickly stops about 20 yards ahead of the accident. Five young men, all wearing Alabama T-shirts and hats, jump out of the Blazer. They're carrying baseball bats, crowbars, and one golf club... A 7-iron. Mark hands Kevin the stun gun and pepper spray, and he keeps the baton.

"Why do you get to keep the baton?" Kevin complains.

"I gave you all the weapons a bitch would have in her purse. You know, because you go to Ohio State," Mark replies.

"That's THE Ohio State to you! Let's kick these guys asses!" Kevin prepares for battle.

Two of the faster Bama' faithful come running full speed, raising the crowbars over their heads, ready to strike down on the guys. Kevin quickly sprays the pepper spray in one of the rednecks' eyes, blinding him instantly. The other attacker swings at Mark but misses. The blinded man starts swinging wildly in the air and strikes his partner's head, splitting it wide open. He swings again and connects with the man's nose and mouth. Blood sprays all over Kevin's face and chest.

"Yes, I got you son-of-a-bitch." The sightless man says he is proud of his accomplishment.

One of the other men from the truck, heavy set and carrying the 7-iron, quickly approaches the group. Kevin aims and fires his stun gun, connecting with the man's chest and causing him to fall to the ground.

"Take that, you John Daly-looking motherfucker!" Kevin shouts, thinking the man resembles the former pro golfer.

Mark strikes the wildly swinging blind man with the baton in the throat. He falls instantly to his knees and gasps for air from his broken larynx. Mark walks over to the shocked and woozy "golfer" and cracks him over the head with the baton.

The last two men from the truck arrive at the brawl. Kevin's struck in the arm with a baseball bat, and he drops the can of pepper spray. The man kicks the pepper spray can out of Kevin's reach. Instead, Kevin picks up the 7-iron, gives his best impression of the *Happy Gilmore* swing from the movie, and directly hits the man's balls. He falls to the ground in crippling pain, as any man would.

Mark and the last man of the group are engaged in what resembles a terrible reenactment of the fencing match between the *Dread Pirate Roberts* and *Inigo Montoya* from the film "Princess Bride" with their bat and baton. They're along the roadside, and out of nowhere, an orange pickup truck runs straight into *Inigo Montoya*, sending him flying into the windshield of the crashed police car, killing him instantly. A college-aged man sticks his head and arms out the window, looking back at Mark, and screams, "Hook 'em Horns!" while holding up his fist with his hands formed into the famous University of Texas hand sign that resembles a bull. The back of the truck has a Texas Longhorns bumper sticker.

Kevin makes one last swing at the man clutching his nuts and knocks him out with a blow to the head.

"Holy shit, now we have Texas and Auburn to thank for helping us out. I think everyone hates Alabama," Mark suggests.

"Yeah, at least they weren't Penn State fans. I can't be thankful for them," Kevin replies.

"Finally, we agree on something," Mark says.

They grab some of the weapons and walk over to the white Blazer. The keys are in the ignition, and the engine is still running. They throw the weapons in the back seat and jump in.

The Big Ten rivals sit briefly to catch their breath and calm down. Kevin puts the vehicle in drive and heads down the lonely road in the same direction as the Texas boys, who are no longer in sight. Kevin notices the gas tank is nearly empty and has yet to learn where the next gas station is.

"Fuck, we're going to run out of gas soon," Kevin informs.

"Let's drive to the next farmhouse and ask for some gas. I'm sure these hick farmers have some in their barns," Mark suggests.

"Dude, you haven't noticed that everyone in this area wants to kill us? The word has probably spread all over the state on their Ham radios and C.B.s." Kevin responds.

"I'll stay in the truck, you take off your shirt, and you'll blend right in as a fat shirtless redneck, or what I like to call a Buckeye," Mark says.

"First, I'm not fat. Second, I'm not a redneck, and third I can't take off my shirt because I have a huge OSU tat on my chest," Kevin says as he lifts his shirt to expose the tattoo.

"Are you fucking kidding me?" Mark replies, lifting his shirt and exposing his giant Michigan "M" on his chest.

"I would say that great minds think alike, but great minds don't come from Michigan," Kevin quips in response to the similar tattoos.

"Hey, look at that house. The Texas guy's orange truck is out front. They'll help us out," Marks notices.

Kevin turns the Blazer up the long dirt driveway and parks next to the orange pickup truck. There's nobody in sight. They exit the vehicle and walk to the porch and front door. Mark knocks loudly, and Kevin stands ready for anything. An older man answers the door.

"Can I help you boys?" He asks cautiously.

"Hey, old-timer, we ran out of gas and wondered if you could spare any. We thought maybe you had some in the barn or somewhere," Kevin asks.

"Sure do. I have a couple of cans in my shed that I can give you. Come on in, and my Millie will make you some fresh lemonade. It's the best in the state. She won an award in the county fair for it last year," the old man says proudly.

The guys enter the house, observing everything and looking for signs of trouble. The old man tells his wife, sitting in her favorite chair reading the book *"Tales from the H1d3away"*, to get two glasses of lemonade. She gets up and heads to the kitchen. Mark and Kevin take a seat on the couch.

"We don't want to be a burden, sir. We'll be out of your hair quickly," Kevin says.

"Nonsense, boys. The name's Harold. We don't get visitors around here much, but it's always nice to see some friendly faces," Harold replies.

"What about the two young guys who drive the orange truck? Where are they? I want to thank them for helping us down the road," Marks asks.

"Those are my two boys. They're out doing their chores in the barn and field," Harold answers.

Millie returns with a green pitcher and pours two large, refreshing-looking lemonades. They take their glasses and start drinking the sweet, sugary drink.

"Holy crap, I can see why this is an award winner," Kevin says.

A couple hours later, Mark and Kevin wake up from their drug-induced sleep. They try to move but are tied up and in the house's basement. Mark starts to shout for help, and Kevin joins in. They hear Harold's voice coming from the dark corner of the basement.

"Nobody's going to hear you way out here and from my basement?" Harold says.

"What the fuck do you want from us? We didn't do anything to you? We just want to get to the game and then return home," Kevin pleads.

Millie walks into the room wearing an Alabama T-shirt, and Harold appears behind them wearing an LSU jersey.

"Oh fuck, you're the old couple from the Fiesta Bowl in Phoenix," Kevin recalls.

"Nice to see you again. I don't think you boys will be making the game, but you'll still get to see it," Harold replies with a sinister giggle.

"Where are your sons? Why did they bother to help us if you're just going to kill us?" Mark inquires.

"I lied; they're not my sons. They were drunk frat boys looking for a place to sleep it off for the night. However, I was truthful about their location in the barn. I shot them both in the face with my shotgun and fed them to the hogs," Harold confesses.

"Just like we're going to do to you both," Millie says with a creepy laugh, jumping up and down and clapping.

"Nah, I got something different planned for these two Big Ten shitheads. You get to live a couple more days, and more importantly, you'll still get to watch the game," Harold says.

Mark and Kevin have been tied to uncomfortable wooden chairs for two days. Harold and Millie are now standing in front of them. An old Zenith television is on a small stand beside the older man. He turns to the channel of the championship game, and the reception is terrible due to the antenna broadcast.

"Sorry, boys. That's the best we can get for the game. We don't have cable or satellite or any of those surge services for better reception," Harold explains.

"They call them streaming services, Harold," Millie corrects him.

"I don't give a fuck what they call them. Here's what's going to happen, boys. Whichever team wins, that fan gets a peaceful death. However, you'll have to shoot the other one in the kneecaps before dying. Then, after a few minutes, you can shoot him in the head to end his suffering," Harold explains.

"You're a couple of crazy old fuckers still stuck in the 1920s," Kevin says with anger and fear in his voice.

"Do we look like we're over 100 years old, dumbshit?" Millie responds, offended by missing her age by about 20 years.

"Yes, yes you do," Kevin replies.

"Kevin shut up. Look, Harold and Millie, we're just fans of college teams we attended, like you. We don't control who wins or loses. Alabama and LSU are great schools and will be in the running for a championship next year. How about we have some delicious lemonade, a drug-free version, and watch the game together? No more killing," Mark pleads.

"Did you try that big college psychology mind game on me, boy? I have a degree in engineering and agriculture from

LSU, and my Millie has a teaching degree from Bama'. We're not dumb hick farmers, son," Harold reveals.

"I didn't think you were, and I'm not trying anything. I don't see the point in killing us over college football games. Well, I understand killing him because it is Ohio State," Mark replies, gesturing with his head at Kevin.

"Because it's Alabama, there is no other school. Roll Tide!" Millie shouts. "Roll Tide!" Harold repeats.

"Why the fuck are you saying roll tide, and how are you still alive in Alabama country as an LSU fan?" Kevin asks.

"My heart lies with Bama'. I got expelled in 1963 for punching a professor that got his degree from fucking Florida State. So, I had to finish at LSU. Millie has a lot of pull around here for being a school teacher who taught just about every person in these parts, so as her husband and brother, they're okay with me being an LSU alum, but it's Bama' first, Roll Tide!" Harold answers. "Roll Tide!" Millie repeats.

"Of course, you're also brother and sister," Kevin says.

"The game's about to start. It's time to shut the hell up and watch. Here's some lemonade for all of us. Yes, this time, it will be drug-free. We need you awake," Millie cuts them off as she pours lemonade from a red pitcher into four glasses.

"What a game! It's an instant classic that will be rewatched over and over. You can tell both teams came to play and win; it's just sad one team had to lose," the sports announcer says.

"Unbelievable. What an electric atmosphere. I feel sorry for anybody who didn't experience this game in person. Our T.V. broadcast was incredible, but to be here is something special. It was the best college football game I've ever witnessed," the other sports announcer adds.

Harold gets out of an old recliner and turns off the T.V. Millie grabs the pistol that the victorious fan will use to shoot the other one. Harold stands behind the winner with his shotgun pointed at his head to prevent him from trying to shoot them instead of his Big Ten rival. Millie unties one arm of the shooter, hands the gun to him, and goes next to Harold.

"Hell of a game, buddy. I'm sorry, but it will be our last one together," Mark tells Kevin.

"Yeah, that was the best game I'd ever seen. I'm actually glad I got to watch it with you. You're not bad for a Michigan fan," Kevin replies.

"Yeah, yeah, great game. Whatever, just hurry up and shoot him in the knees, or I'll blow your head off and shoot him myself," Harold says impatiently.

The Big Ten victorious fan raises the gun and aims at his rival's kneecap. He's trembling and doesn't want to shoot, but he understands he has to. He's in no position to turn and shoot the old couple without getting a head full of buckshot.

Bang! Bang! Two loud blasts echo through the basement.

Kevin's face is sprayed with blood and brain fragments, and the old couple drops dead from gunshots to the head. Kevin and Mark are startled by the shots that didn't come from the pistol or Harold's shotgun.

"You two okay down here. We came here as quickly as we could. Do you know where the senator's son is?" a man on the stairs dressed in a suit asks.

"Huh? Who are you, and what the fuck just happened?" Kevin asks.

"I'm Agent John Simmons of the FBI. We tracked the senator's son's truck here. He's been missing for two days," he asks.

"Hogs got em'!" Kevin replies.

"Hogs? Do you mean Arkansas Razorback fans or the Mega Moo sorority?" Agent Simmons asks.

"No sir, he means the hogs in the barn got them. The old man told us he shot the Texas boys and fed them to the hogs," Mark explains.

"Dammit, we're too late. However, it appears we're just in time for you guys. It looked like you were about to shoot him when I came in?" Agent Simmons says.

"Please untie us so we can get out of this fucking house of horrors. Those two old fucks were insane," Kevin says.

Agent Simmons helps both men out of their restraints and stands them up. They're both wobbly from sitting so long in the same position. A few other agents are securing the house and its grounds. One of the agents gathers the weapons lying on the ground. He unloads the shotgun first and then moves on to the pistol.

"Huh, this pistol isn't even loaded. Not sure why they handed you an empty gun?" The agent questions.

Kevin and Mark look at each other and conclude that Harold was about to blow their heads off anyway.

"It's a shame you couldn't make it to the game. They're already calling it one of the greatest games ever. Although I hate both teams, we listened on the radio on the way here. I went to a real school, Michigan State," Agent Simmons says jokingly.

"Agent Simmons, If you're thirsty, that crazy bitch made some award-winning lemonade. It's in the green pitcher in the fridge," Mark says as they walk upstairs to the fresh Alabama air.

SECTION 218

There are many difficult situations or obstacles in the sports world for players, such as trying to throw a perfect game in baseball, repeating as champions, and overcoming adversity. Over the years, we've also seen examples of hard times that the sports fan has to endure, such as greedy team owners moving their teams to another city for money and a new stadium, leaving loyal fans without a team. The agony of watching your favorite player go down with a season-ending injury in week one. The team's star player getting traded to a rival team at the trade deadline. Whatever the pain, every team suffers, and every fan feels it, some more than others. This isn't new to the sports world. There are two sides to the sports fan, winners and losers. Both sides of the sports team fan spectrum are a competition in and of itself. One side, the successful one, will brag about how good their team is compared to other well-performing teams. The other side will vent (and brag) about how bad their team is and develop a sense of pride if their team is the worst. People will argue, "No way, our team is much worse than yours!" or "I hope we keep losing to get the first draft pick." However, nothing is more complex or challenging than this one element in the sports world...

Being a Detroit Lions fan is a birthright, an inheritance, and a curse. After all, nobody from outside of Michigan chooses to be a Lions fan. Well, at least nobody sane. The pain and agony of cheering for our beloved Lions has become routine and expected. There used to be the argument that the Chicago Cubs fans are the most miserable, but they ruined that title after the Cubs finally won the World Series in 2016. The Detroit Lions have only won one playoff game during the entire Superbowl era that started in 1967. I've known this pain for over 50 years, so I'm an expert. However, this story isn't about me, 10-year season ticket holder section 218, row S, seats 1 and 2. This tale is about Paul Faraday, a 21-year season ticket holder in section 218, row R, seats 1 and 2, and possibly the Detroit Lion's number one fan.

Paul owns a construction company that received the winning bid to build all of the stadium stairs in the brand-new *Rocket Mortgage Stadium,* or what the Detroit fans call it... *The Den.* The team's stadium in downtown Detroit was built after the Ford family sold the team to the winning bidder, Detroit native son and billionaire Dan Gilbert. He beat out fellow billionaire and adult content streaming giant Sid Sanderson for the ownership of the sports franchise.

For Paul's excellent work in helping to rebuild and restore Detroit and his 30 years of loyalty to the team, he was awarded two seats of his choosing for life by the new team president and former Lions great Barry Sanders. These seats are suitable for all Lion's home games and all other events held in the stadium. Now, you're probably saying, *"Why didn't he pick a better area than section 218, Row R, seats 1 and 2?"* which is located around the 35-yard line, second level. There's a particular reason Paul had to have these seats. He wanted to watch the results of his *"masterpiece,"* which he calls "The Mis-Step," during Lions home games and events.

During construction, Paul and a couple of his supervisors thought it would be hilarious to have one step ½ way up in section 218, one inch higher than the rest. This one "Mis-Step" is an unnoticeable difference to the naked eye from the other 75 steps in that long climb to the top. *What makes that so special?* You ask.

Anyone who has ever made that journey up stadium stairs to their seats knows it can be quite the hike. Most people get a rhythm when they ascend to their row and assigned seat, but a step one inch higher than others makes for great entertainment. Paul understood that when he designed "The Mis-Step," so, he chose section 218, row R, Seats 1 and 2, to enjoy the endless laughs watching people trip over that extra inch of concrete. His seat is two rows higher than "The Mis-Step," which gives him a perfect view of victims tripping and falling. I'm behind him, so I get the same pleasure when it happens. I may have been a victim of the treacherous step once or twice.

Like every true Detroit Lions fan, Paul is loyal to his team. Through the good times... Well, I should say only through the bad times; they haven't had any good times since the 1950s. He loves all of his Detroit sports teams but favors the Lions. They're the only Detroit team in the four major sports leagues he hasn't seen win a championship. He was a teenager when the Tigers won the World Series in 1984. Partying in college when the Pistons won championships in 1989 and 90 (and again in 2004). He celebrated watching the Red Wings win four championships in the 1990s and early 2000s. He's even watched his alma mater, the University of Michigan, win football, hockey, and basketball championships.

Paul often brings a family member, coworker, or good friend to share his other season ticket to the games. Today, he brought his wife, Jennifer Faraday, with him, section 218, row R, seat 2. Jennifer is a huge football fan and really gets into it. She's been to the most games with him and is equally amused at the unsuspecting climbing victims. The Lions are preparing to kick off, and the fans are getting loud.

"This has to be the year they win it all. I've seen all my teams win a championship, so if the Lions win the Super Bowl, I can finally die happy," Paul tells his wife.

"Hell, Yay, we're winning this whole damn thing!" She shouts and starts high-fiving everyone around her. "Besides, if they don't win a Super Bowl, I might kill you anyway," she jokes.

"Hold on, here comes one! Wait for it... Wait for it...!" Paul yells out to those around him who know about the secret of "The Mis-Step."

They all watch in anticipation of what is about to transpire. A man in his late 20s holding a full beer in each hand while climbing the stairs to his seat somewhere above. He has a steady groove going, with an excited smile from the anticipation of today's game and the energy from the crowd. He has no idea what lies ahead of him in five steps: 4, 3, 2, 1...

"BOOM!" the crowd chants.

I admit that the few knowledgeable section 218 fans, including my wife and me, all crack up at once as the young man trips on "The Mis-Step," and both beers fly out of his hands onto the steps above him, the area we call "The Splash Zone."

The man wasn't fast enough to brace for his fall, so he hit his head on the steps, slightly cracking it open. The fans laugh at his misfortunes as he stands up woozy from his collision with the concrete step. He tries to hide his embarrassment through laughter and waving to everyone. I wonder what stings more, the small bleeding gash on his forehead or the $40 he spent on those two large, delicious-looking IPA beers he once held in those happy hands. He'll have to report back empty-handed to whoever should have received one of those two beverages.

"Fuck yay! That was awesome. Look at his head; it's bleeding!" Jennifer yells out while laughing and pointing at the man.

"Who won the 'Blood Pot'?" A man from row T, seat 4 or 5, yells out.

Paul pulls a folded paper from his pocket and opens it. He scans the paper for the information being requested.

"Freddie, row P, seat 3. He had *chosen 'before the game started'* as his winning pick for the first blood pot. Congrats, $22 for you, sir. Okay, everyone playing, put in your $2 for the next one," Paul requested from the "Blood Pot" participants.

He wouldn't be the only spectator we've seen lose their drinks or food items or shed some blood over this past inaugural season. My favorite was a large Chicago Bears fan a month ago during halftime. He was returning to his seat a few rows above us with a large beer and hot dog in hand. He had a confident "victory" smirk because his team led at halftime 14-10. Due to his weight, he could not jog up the steps, but he maintained a rhythm that we all knew would lead to disaster. The anticipation was as exciting as a last-minute game-winning drive. He reached "The Mis-Step" and...

"Boom"!!! The crowd chants.

We even felt the entire section shake like an earthquake had just occurred. The beer managed to land on the big man's head, and the hot dog, with plenty of mustard, found his face as he tumbled down the stairs about seven rows. His black sweatpants managed to end up around his knees, exposing his white boxers and enormous buttock cleavage. To the fan's surprise, that remarkable fall was captured on camera and shared multiple times on the giant stadium video board during a timeout in the 3ʳᵈ quarter. He received the loudest cheer of the game. The players on both teams were pointing and laughing at the highlight. The Bears would lose 31-17, the best "greatest bad day of his life" moment for that guy.

Paul's favorite moment, which he likes to share with people around him at every game, didn't happen during a Lion's game. He brought his teenage daughter to the Taylor Quick concert about two months ago. He was surrounded by thousands of screaming teenage girls and boys, a few other miserable dads, and several hot MILFS. He knew his only joy would be that glorious step two rows down. The first moment came when two teenage girls tripped and spilled soda all over their brand-new Taylor Quick T-shirts and started crying. After chuckling at several kids falling, the moment he was finally waiting for to make his "*masterpiece*" worth it was just three steps away. A beautiful woman with the most incredible set of fake breasts he's ever seen is carefully hiking up the stairs with two sodas in her hands. His first thought was to warn her about the step, which goes against the "Code of the Mis-Step*." No warning to anyone approaching the Mis-Step; let it play out!*

Her approach was like the slow-motion beach scene in the 1979 film "10," starring Bo Derek. The MILF's breasts bounced in perfect sync with every step in her glowing white tube top. She reaches "The Mis-Step" and trips as expected. She lets go of the sodas to catch herself on the center-hand rail. Paul is impressed that she thinks so quickly about saving herself from hitting the steps that so many others fail to do. However, to Paul's delight, she somehow manages to pull her tube top down, exposing her perfectly round, large, naked breasts right in front of him. The torture of the screaming kids for the past hour was now worth every painful decibel.

She quickly pulls up her tube top, gives Paul a quick, embarrassed smile, and disappears to the top of section 218. Paul looks around the section, and only one fellow miserable dad sitting a couple of seats back witnessed glory. He gives Paul two thumbs up with an enormous cheesy grin for their special bonding moment. Everyone else nearby seemed to have ignored or completely missed what just happened and continues screaming the lyrics of Taylor Quick's song, "Allegedly". Another Billboard top 10 hit about her recent breakup and divorce from her 2nd husband, Samir Nazari.

After one pre-season game, nine regular season games, and their first playoff win at home in over 30 years, the most fantastic day in Detroit has arrived. The Lions are hosting the NFC championship game against the Philadelphia Eagles for the first time in the Superbowl era. The stadium is electric as fans are arriving to their seats. The noise of the sold-out crowd is deafening and much more satisfying to the ears than the screaming teenagers a few months ago at the Taylor Quick concert. The "Let's Go Lions" chant is infinitely better than any of her depressing breakup songs, and the "Honolulu Blue Wave" of Detroit fans is a sight to see.

The NFC championship game in Detroit isn't the only thing about this game that Paul's excited about. Like many others in the country, he truly despises Eagles fans. He wants "The Mis-Step" to welcome them graciously but also painfully.

The first quarter ends with the Lions jumping to a quick 14-0 lead. There were only a few funny moments that "The Mis-Step" caused during the game. Most people in this part of section 218 are privy to its dangers after learning the hard way. Unfortunately, there hasn't been any luck with Eagle fan's introduction to "The Mis-Step," but three-quarters remain.

Finally, during the 4th quarter, Paul's moment came. After realizing the Eagles have no chance at a comeback, being down 24-10 with two minutes left and Detroit with the ball, most of the Philly fans who somehow procured tickets to the game are leaving. The chants of "*Na na na na, na na na na, hey*

hey, goodbye" echo throughout the stadium. Paul's singing voice is booming to some Philly fans descending past him towards the exit. He's practically in their face, letting them know they're no longer welcome in "The Den."

The Philly fans make it a few more rows down before one of the men is struck by a flying beer cup. The cup comes from somewhere behind Paul, but the first face the Philly man locks on to is Paul's mug. The fan immediately assumes that Paul is the beer cup culprit and starts running back up the steps toward him angrily.

Paul is trying to tell the man it wasn't him because he doesn't condone that kind of behavior from fans. He's seen numerous video clips of fans fighting at NFL games on TikTok and is appalled at their actions. He doesn't want to become the same harmful streaming content he hates. However, Paul knows he has an ally that will protect him. The fans nearby watch with anticipation of what's about to happen.

"Boom!" the crowd chants.

The Philly fan never reaches Paul as his face is greeted with concrete steps, knocking a few teeth out. He somehow ends up mangled in the center-hand rail like a human pretzel knot. He takes a minute to unravel from the shining aisle dividers, gathers himself together, and starts his "Walk Of Shame" down the stairs as section 218 laughs at him. The Philly man raises his two bloody hands and points both middle fingers toward the crowd as he leaves. The "friendly" gesture produces more laughs because his right middle finger is broken and bent sideways at the knuckle. His embarrassment and, most likely, his drunkenness causes him to be unaware of his injuries. He disappears into the exit tunnel but remains forever in our memories. The party continues in Section 218 as cheers and laughter get louder when the players return to the field after the 2-minute warning timeout.

Paul looks at his wife with tears and a smile as big as the 100-yard field below. Jen loves her Lions, too, but she isn't as obsessed with sports as Paul. Seeing him this happy brings her tears.

"The Lions are going to the Superbowl, Honey Bear!" he shouts with joy in every word.

"Fuck yes, we are! You're getting a special blowjob tonight!" Jen shouts with joy, and Paul's excitement doubles.

Everyone nearby is high-fiving, hugging, and fist-bumping each other with the realization they're a part of history… It will be the first Superbowl appearance by the Detroit Lions.

Detroit Lions fans have a few options to watch their beloved team this Sunday while they battle to become Superbowl champions. They can fork over thousands of dollars and try to get tickets to the game in Los Angeles at SoFi stadium, not including the travel costs. The most popular option is to watch the game on the TV while attending or hosting a Superbowl party. However, for 65,000 Lions fanatics, the best choice is to participate in the viewing party at "The Den."

Season ticket holders, like Paul and I, had the first choice of whether to attend or give up their seats. It was a no-brainer for most of us. The viewing party sold out within an hour. The place is going to be packed and full of excitement. The game will be challenging since they're taking on the defending Superbowl champs, the Miami Dolphins. Their star tight end, Trevor Kacey, is dating Taylor Quick. I'm sure that the Fox Sports producers already have a camera directed at her luxury box suite to show the world every reaction she has when Trevor touches the ball. Paul is disappointed he'll have to see her pompous face again after only a few months on the big screen in "The Den."

Finally, the day is here. "The Den" is jumping with excitement, activities, and music. The game will begin soon, and the stands are nearly full. A few dozen former Detroit Lions are sitting in the VIP section on the field. They're waving and walking around, signing autographs to the lucky fans in the front rows. I can't help but notice something missing from all this electric buzz. Paul's two seats remain empty. *Did he end up*

getting tickets to the Super Bowl? Is he hosting a party at home?
I hope that he isn't missing the game for any reason.

Suddenly, only a minute before kick-off, Paul and his wife Jen appear from the entrance tunnel and begin the climb to their seats. Everyone who knows the popular couple in Section 218 is relieved to see them ascending toward Row R and taking their cherished seats. Everyone cheered them on, and Paul didn't expect such a warm welcome. He stands with tears in his eyes and gives a humble bow.

Jen stands next to him, smiles, and waves to the crowd. She leans over to Paul and whispers, "Sit the fuck down, King Paul. The game is starting, so stop making this about you. If you jinx this game, no special blowjobs for a year."

Paul immediately sits down.

Just 5 minutes into the game, Detroit scores first with a 29-yard touchdown pass from star quarterback Jeremy Groff. "The Den" erupts louder than ever until 2 minutes later when the Lion's defense intercepts the ball and scores. The stadium is deafening. Paul, like many other fans, has already lost their voice from yelling and screaming. Only one minute remains in the half, and Trevor Kacey catches his first pass. Fox Sports captures footage of Taylor Quick jumping and cheering in her luxury suite. "The Den" erupts in a loud chorus of "Boo's"! The first half ends with Miami kicking a field goal.

Halftime: Detroit 17, Miami 3

During the 3rd quarter, the Lions played poorly, allowing Miami to mount a small comeback. "The Den" is much quieter and more nervous. The 3rd quarter ends with Miami driving down to the Detroit 38-yard line and trailing only 20-17.

However, just three plays into the 4th quarter, the crowd noise and excitement dramatically return after the Miami Dolphins running back fumbles the ball, and Detroit recovers. The Lions need eight plays to score another touchdown and go up by 10 points. Nobody in Section 218 will dare say, "It's over!" or "We're going to win!" that is the ultimate jinx, and you'll probably get your ass kicked. Lion's fans don't want the label of being the "BLG"... the Bad Luck Guy (or Girl).

The 4th quarter is coming to an end, and the Dolphins have the ball but are down by four points, 27-23. They need a touchdown to win. Trevor Kacey catches a 16-yard pass and gets out of bounds. Another camera shot of Taylor Quick for the 14th time during the game.

"BOOOOOOO!" "The Den!" shouts for the 14th time.

However, Paul thinks about those amazing naked breasts of the concert tube top woman every time they show the superstar diva on the screen, so his "boos" aren't as loud.

Miami is on Detroit's 19-yard line, with a 4th down and only 11 seconds left. They are out of timeouts, so this will likely be the final play of the game. Everyone in "The Den" is standing and watching intensely.

The ball is snapped.

Miami's young star quarterback, Blake Powers, falls back.

He scrambles to his right from the defensive pressure.

Blake throws it towards the end zone.

The ball soars through the air for what feels like an eternity.

It's caught!

Detroit has intercepted the ball, and there are no penalty flags. The Detroit Lions are Superbowl champions for the first time in franchise history. "The Den" erupts, and madness is everywhere. Tears, screams, and pure joy fill the stadium like never before. Paul turns around and gives me a huge hug. He runs down the stairs several rows, high-fiving any extended hand that comes his way. Paul goes over to the other side of the rail and runs back up, high-fiving everyone on the aisle in Section 219. He is overjoyed and might have a permanent smile tattooed on his face.

Paul sees another fan a few rows up, standing with his arms open to embrace him as he approaches. He picks up the pace to greet the fellow Detroiter, but the one-inch menace, "The Mis-Step," catches Paul's left foot, and he falls head first into the concrete stairs.

"You fucking idiot!" Jen shouts while laughing along with everyone else in the section.

The new NFL season kicks off in a few minutes, with Detroit playing the Las Vegas Raiders on Thursday night. The team will raise its championship banner right before game time. The place is completely full except for two seats... Section 218, Row R, Seats 1 and 2. I look down at the empty chair in front of me, seat 1, and read the freshly engraved plaque...

In Memoriam
Paul Faraday
"Loyal Fan"

The End.

THE NFX-33

This will be the 4th annual car race across America known as "The NetFux 3300" or "The NFX-33" for short. The eccentric multi-billionaire, playboy, and car enthusiast Sid Sanderson created the popular once-a-year event. The name derives from two parts: The first part comes from the race's sponsor and exclusive televised coverage, *NetFux*, which is the world's largest porn streaming company. The second part comes from the race's total miles from its starting point in Miami, Florida, to the finish line in Seattle, Washington, approximately 3,300 miles.

Sid created *NetFux* in 2008 after realizing that streaming services would eventually replace DVDs. He earned his bachelor's degree in business from UCLA and his MBA from USC while working in porn to pay for his tuition. He became an international porn star by producing and performing characters such as *Bruce Willie* in the porno action movies; "Lie Hard," "Lie Harder," and "Lie Hardest." His eighth, ninth, and twelfth films, respectively. Once he retired from banging female terrorists and saving the world, on camera, that is, he used his business degrees and porn-star money to create *NetFux*. By 2020, the streaming service had over 100 million subscribers worldwide.

Sid is #29 on Forbes Magazines' top 50 most eligible bachelors worldwide. His salt-and-pepper hair, finely shaved beard, and athletic 6'2" frame provide no struggle with dating the ladies. Of course, his money and porn star past help, too. After all, there's no hiding what he's packing under his pants. He has never been married or fathered any children. Sid decided to get a vasectomy during his porn days to avoid unwanted pregnancies.

"The NetFux 3300" was inspired by Sid's love for cars and one of his favorite 1980's movies, "The Cannonball Run," which starred his all-time favorite actor, Dom DeLuise, as *Captain Chaos*. He could have bought a racing team in NASCAR and tried once to own a Formula One team but was outbid. Sid decided he wanted something new, exciting, and risky. The race isn't strictly legal, and the drivers can get pulled over if caught by the police.

Sid owns a warehouse in Las Vegas where he houses the world's most extensive collection of *Matchbox* and *Hot Wheels* die-cast toy cars. He's collected the popular toys since he was three years old and was only allowed to open a select few to conduct make-believe races. His dad made him keep most of the cars in their original packaging to increase their value over time, and the rumor is that his toy car collection is worth somewhere north of $38,000,000. He's always favored the *Hot Wheels* version of KITT, his limited edition *1982 Pontiac Firebird Trans Am* replica from his favorite TV show in the 1980s, "Knight Rider." He still carries it in his pocket to this day. Although, due to wear and tear over the years, its monetary value is worthless, its emotional value is priceless.

The race is held every Labor Day weekend from Thursday to Monday. Sid secretly selects the eleven vehicle models; however, the rumor is that he conducts a *Matchbox* vs. *Hot Wheel* tournament in his warehouse to determine that year's car models. The contestants and their vehicles get chosen by a drawing they entered earlier in the year during a live televised special on *NetFux* a month before the race. The eleven teams consist of two cars and two drivers per team in the selected make and model for that race. Each year, the types of vehicles are different, except for the previous year's winner, who gets to defend their title. This year's competitors consist of the following vehicles and their team names:

1. Ford F-150s- "The Whitey Fords"
2. Honda Odyssey- "The KarenVans"
3. Chevrolet Corvette- "Mid-Life Crisis" (Last year's winners)
4. Telsa Model 3- "The MUSKeteers"
5. Jeep Wranglers- "Jeepers Creepers"
6. Ford Focus- "Hocus Focus"
7. Volkswagen Bus- "The Streetful Dead"
8. Volkswagen Jetta- "Wokeswagen"
9. Toyota Prius- "Rainbow Power"
10. Porsche 911 Carrera- "The Good Nine 11"

11. Mini Cooper S- "The British Invasion"

The object of the race is for all vehicles to depart from *The Hard Rock Stadium's* parking lot in Miami, Florida, at 7:11 p.m. Sid's an avid craps player, on Thursday evening. They will travel 3,300 miles across the country, any route they choose, to arrive at the finish line at *Lumen Field* in Seattle, Washington. The teams cannot travel from midnight to 6:00 a.m. and must pull over for rest.

The first team with at least one vehicle crossing the finish line is declared the victor and will receive a trophy and $1,000,000 for each team member. Every year, the race faces many obstacles, such as the police, traffic, weather, fans, etc. The teams and vehicle brands are no longer given to the media in advance due to the most significant issue, the race's popularity. Last year, one of the Subaru Outback "Plant Based" team members were run off the road by show fans trying to get selfies while driving alongside them. The teams are now top secret but will become a target once the race starts and is televised on *NetFux*.

The twenty-two drivers and their vehicles are all in place for the start of this year's "NFX-33." They are inspecting their vehicles and the competition. The podium where Sid will address the teams is empty except for a couple of security personnel, a menacing black female dwarf, and an IT guy setting up the microphone. The teams are going over their strategies and smack-talking their competitors next to them.

"You middle-aged dads are going down this year. Don't you have a lame sports bar to go to and order the beef nachos and some off-the-wall silly named micro-brewed IPA?" Brad from the team "The Good Nine 11" jokes.

"When does your grandma die? So you can get the remainder of your trust fund money?" Scotty Braun of "Mid-Life Crisis" returns fire.

Sid, escorted by the black female dwarf and some VIPs, walks onto the stage and takes their seats. Sid approaches the microphone and pauses before speaking to scan the crowd of fans, media, and racers. The drivers and spectators go crazy with a standing ovation for the famous billionaire creator of this incredible race. He raises both hands enthusiastically to build up the crowd's excitement to another level. He leans into the microphone.

"Welcome competitors, fans, media, and the wonderful sponsors behind me. This year's race is going to be our biggest and best. I want to quote one of the greatest movies of all time; 'You are certainly the most distinguished group of highway scofflaws and degenerates gathered together in one place.'" He delivers the beginning of his opening monolog.

"What the fuck movie is that from?" Ben, a young man in his early twenties from team "Hocus Focus," asks.

"I know everything about movies. That was clearly from *2 Fast 2 Furious*, the second installment of the magnificent *Fast and Furious* franchise," Preston, also in his early twenties and the second member of Hocus Focus, replies.

They are parked next to "The KarenVans," two middle-aged white women wearing yoga pants and pink workout shirts that read "I like wine and maybe 3 people" and "Death to the Zinfandel." They're both driving grey Honda Odysseys with personalized plates that read; "SUPRMOM" and "TAXI MA". The vehicles also have the Disney family vinyl decals and their child's elementary school honor roll bumper stickers in the back window.

"It's from *Cannonball Run*, Sid's favorite movie. Why the fuck are you Gen Z idiots even here? Don't you have a TikTok video to make?" Answers Karen #1, from "The KarenVans".

"Hey, easy mid-day Target shopper, they're probably the same TikTok videos you sit and watch instead of paying attention to your family during Disney movie night," Preston quips back.

Sid concludes his speech, and the drivers begin to get antsy, knowing the race is about to start. They must wait for Sid's signals to begin. At this point, the strategies of each team are implemented. Some teams will quickly race out, and others will take their time avoiding the cluster fuck that will happen exiting the stadium.

"One last thing before you start your journey... 'Think of the fact that there's not one state in the 50 that has the death penalty for speeding... Although I'm not sure about..." Sid ends his speech with the crowd yelling the finishing movie line quote ... "OHIO!"

"That's also a quote from *Cannonball Run*, Dawson Creek!" Karen #1 sarcastically tells the team, "Hocus Pocus."

"Who the fuck is *Dawson Creek*?" Ben whispers to Preston.

"I don't know, I'm still trying to figure out what the fuck *Cannonball Run* is," Preston replies.

Sid waves the green flag, and the mad dash begins. Drivers jump into their vehicles and quickly leave, nearly causing a few fender benders. The more patient teams are still parked. Some are going over game plans with each other, and some are just chilling and listening to music. The Volkswagen Bus team, "The Streetful Dead," climbs into one of the VW buses, and a minute later, a large cloud of smoke exits all the cracked windows.

Sid speaks to his VIPs, looks out at the beginning mayhem of his creation, and then walks off stage to his limousine. The drivers will see him again at the race's conclusion at *Lumen Field*'s parking lot in Seattle, Washington.

There is a team of sports announcers calling the race live on *NetFux*. The race coverage is captured by *NetFux's* small army of news helicopters, two sexy roving reporters, and their two cameramen. The television in-studio hosts are Marvel Spencer, one of Sid's long-time porn co-stars, and Seth Kowalski, his favorite standup comedian.

The first lovely roving reporter that will interview teams at stops across the country is Ashlee "Candee Cane" Sundberg, a porn star that had one scene with him in his 2nd adult film, "Thighway to Hell." She played a demon woman trying to seduce Sid's character, *Father Richards*. She's now a 3rd-grade teacher in Rancho Cucamonga, California, but she moonlights for him as a reporter during special events.

The second is Tara "Minxy" Anders, a former adult film star who co-starred with Sid in eight of his Twelve pornographic films. Agent Connie Lingis was her most famous role in the "Lie Hard" trilogy. She's now a well-known social media influencer and the lead choreographer for American rapper *Lizzo*. She's the only woman Sid has asked for her hand in marriage… six times. She doesn't love him that way but enjoys working gigs for him and is suitable for a random shag when she needs it. The foursome will provide play-by-play, recaps, interviews, backstories of the drivers, and live updates.

Nearly all *NetFux* subscribers tune in for the four-day race. Marvel and Seth begin their commentary after Sid starts the race.

"The race has officially begun, and the first one out of the parking lot is Thomas Harris from Birmingham, England, on team 'The British Invasion,' driving one of the Mini Coopers." Marvel Spencer updates the television audience.

"Oh shit, we got a *peaky fucking blinder* in the race. Better just let Thomas Shelby win. Sorry, I just started binge-watching that show. So good!" Seth Kowalski jokes in a poorly attempted English accent.

"Damn good show, but the driver's name is Thomas Harris, not Shelby like in the show," Marvel laughs.

"Hey, was that Lil' Tea Money on the stage with Sid?" Seth asks.

"Sure was Seth. She's now Sid's head of security. You don't want to mess with her. I had a sex scene with her in 'Big Trousers in Little Jhina,'" Marvel answers.

"I remember that. Your cock in her stubby little black hands looked like she was holding a white birch log," Seth jokes.

"Sorry, Seth, but we already have our first breaking news update. Team 'Hocus Focus', driving the Ford Focus, is already out of the competition. Candee Cane, please report," Marvel says.

"Well, what did you expect? They're driving a Ford Focus, and it's as if they don't want to get laid. Seriously, who drives a Ford Focus? The two cars aren't starting and appear to have gone limp, and everyone knows I don't like it limp," Candee Cane reports with a sultry smile.

"The KarenVans" pass by Candee Cane and the stranded "Hocus Focus" drivers. Karen #1 yells out her vehicle window as she drives by them, "Now you have more time for Fortnite, fucking twinks!"

"See how much you know 50 shades of stupid. Nobody cool plays Fortnite anymore!" Ben yells back at her.

"Nobody cool ever played Fortnite!" she replies.

The two continue trying to get their vehicles to start, and Candee Cane is trying to interview Ben, but he rolls up his window and starts pounding on his steering wheel while yelling obscenities.

"Oh, come on, honey! There's nothing to be afraid of; I don't bite… much," Candee Cane says, peering through Ben's car window.

Preston is sobbing in his vehicle as Candee Cane tries to approach him. He quickly rolls up his window to avoid the sexy reporter.

"Catch up, David, and get that camera focused on my good side. Is this your first gig?" Candee Cane belittles her cameraman, David.

"I was a war photographer and cameraman. I know what I'm doing," he replies.

"Nobody cares, and don't talk, David. This isn't war, it's a fucking car race. Now get over here," she follows up with a bossy tone.

The televised coverage quickly cuts back to the guys in the studio.

"Those poor guys, it's probably their first cars, and their parents still pay for their insurance," Marvel adds.

"And their gas money and zit cream," Seth adds.

A few hours have passed, and the teams are approaching the first mandatory midnight rest stop. Most of the drivers have made it around the Gainesville, Florida area. The teams are about 10 to 20 miles apart, except for Keith Michaels from "Mid-Life Crisis". He was pulled over and issued a speeding ticket just before Orlando. The police officer knew he was in the race and took his time, causing Keith a 30-minute delay.

Marvel and Seth are preparing to give their last play-by-play and update on the *NetFux* broadcast before they call it a night. The streaming service will randomly air Sid's twelve pornos over the next four nights from 12 a.m. to 6 a.m. while the race pauses for the night.

"What an exciting first day, Seth! We're down to 10 teams with Ford Focus cars that still need to start the race. One car has already been pulled over for speeding, and our first overnight break starts now," Marvel states.

"Awesome day, Marvel. From what we can tell, Gaylord Edwards and Gaylene Garcia of Team Rainbow Power are in the early lead, pulling over at a truck stop in Alachua, Florida, just north of Gainesville," Seth says.

"I met them before the race; they are a very nice couple. They seemed close, but I'm not sure if they're dating. They are extremely flamboyant and opinionated," Marvel says.

"Bro, they're gay. They drive a Prius, are flamboyant, and speak two volumes louder than everyone else. She's a trainer for the Phoenix Mercury WNBA team, and he's a talent scout for America's Got Talent. Plus, the word gay is in both their names, but the clincher is they decided to pull over at a truck stop! A haven for homosexuals. Not that there's anything wrong with that!" Seth replies.

"Gay or not, let's check in with the beautiful Tara 'Minxy' Anders. It looks like she has the Jeep team, 'Jeepers Creepers'." Marvel says, changing the subject.

Tara and her cameraman, Jake, approach Lori "Eyes" Bellinger and her teammate Christian Hartling of "Jeepers Creepers" as they park outside a Denny's for a late-night dinner before getting some shuteye. Lori's nine dachshunds start going berserk, jumping and barking, in the Jeep at the approaching reporter.

"Lori, Christian, please have a quick minute for the audience. What are your feelings about the race at this juncture? Do we know them now? Do tell," Tara asks dramatically.

"Jeep Jeep Jeep, Jeep Jeep. Jeep Jeep Jeep. Jeep, Jeep Jeep!" Lori answers while Christian smiles and waves at all the vehicles on the main road passing by.

"Vegas has you at 25 to 1 that you'll finish first. What do you think your odds are of being victorious in this epic race with a vehicle that isn't well-known for its speed? I don't believe there will be any off-terrain roads to conquer," Tara asks intensely.

"Jeep, Jeep Jeep Jeep! Jeep Jeep, Jeep Jeep!" Lori answers with an annoyed tone.

Lori and Christian walk into the Denny's, and Tara reports back to Marvel and Seth at the studio.

"There you have it, ladies and gentlemen. The leader of Team "Jeepers Creepers" has informed us that she strongly feels they have an excellent chance to win because Jeep drivers are amiable and loved by all. They will be overlooked by the numerous law enforcement they will encounter during their journey toward history," Tara relays with a flare for the dramatics.

"Two questions Tara. First, those dogs in the Jeep, are they going to be okay while there eating a fucking grand slam breakfast? Second, how the fuck do you know what she said? All I heard was Jeep," Seth replies.

"As always, Excellent questions, Seth. Lori left the Jeep running with the air conditioning and a water bowl for the weenies. To answer your second question, I once owned a gorgeous red Jeep Wrangler. Therefore, even though my Jeep translation is a bit rusty, I could confidently comprehend what she was communicating to us, allowing me to accurately relay the information to the audience," Tara answers.

The television feed cuts away from Tara and displays only Marvel and Seth with the *NetFux* logo behind them.

"Thank you, Tara, for that interview before we close the broadcast. That Christian guy sure does embrace the 'Jeep Wave' that all Jeepers are known for, doesn't he?" Marvel says.

"Yeah, but I'm pretty sure you're supposed to wave to other Jeeps, not every fucking car on the road like a used car salesman," Seth replies.

A short pause and both men start to laugh.

"Well, Seth, the first day is in the books. I'll see you back here bright and early tomorrow morning to start day two," Marvel says to finish the broadcast.

"Yeah, great, I have to be back here in 5 fucking hours. We comedians are used to late nights but sleep until at least 2 p.m.

"Hey Seth, how many wiener dogs do you think she has in that Jeep?" Marvel asks.

"A hundred," Seth replies.

Marvel laughs as the broadcast ends, and *NetFux* immediately cuts to the start of Sid's fourth porn film, "Shaving Ryan's Privates."

Just outside of Gainesville, Big Willy Donaldson of team "Whitey Ford," in his raised white Ford F-150, leaves the gas station after a late start at 6:27 a.m. Some drivers fill up before midnight, and others do it at 6:00 a.m. He slows down when he notices to his right that both members of the Telsa team, "The MUSKeteers," are at the back of a long line of Teslas at the four supercharging stations. He knows they're stuck there for at least an hour.

"Fucking idiots! That's why you drive a pure Detroit muscle truck like Big Bertha here. Pussy ass electric cars," he validates his vehicle choice to himself.

Suddenly, every Tesla owner exits their vehicle at the same time: 6:28 a.m. They all wear white robes and gather in a semicircle around the giant Tesla logo at the charging station. They get down on their knees and start chanting in a praying position to worship Tesla creator Elon Musk's birthday on June 28th. Weed smokers have their "take a hit" at 4:20 every day, and Tesla owners have their "worship Elon" at 6:28 every day.

Big Willy pulls over to the side of the road and rolls down his window to listen to what the Tesla owners are chanting.

"In Musk, we trust! In Musk, we trust! In Musk, we trust! In Musk, we trust!"

"Yeah, that's some fucking creepy Heaven's Gate cult shit right there. I'm leaving before they have me fuck a goat while they bathe in the blood of a virgin sacrifice," he says.

Just before Big Willy rolls the window back up and leaves, he notices the chanting has suddenly stopped. The Elon Musk disciples kiss, touch, and remove each other's robes, revealing nothing underneath.

"Hold on, this just got interesting," he says while still pulled over to the side of the road to watch the Telsa supercharged sexual orgy launching around the giant logo.

The entire Telsa orgy is captured by *NetFux* news helicopter carrying Candee Cane and her cameraman David.

"So, I guess Telsa stands for: Today Everyone Loves Someone Anonymous. It appears they're a sex cult. That's a bigger orgy than the one that Sid and I did in his fifth film, 'Driving Me's Crazy,' that will be airing tonight right after our broadcast," Marvel says as they begin the day two broadcast.

"That's like a scene from Caligula down there. Watch out for falling upside-down pineapples," Seth jokes.

"Just don't check my browser search history, or you'll find a lot of great content that you can only get here on *NetFux*, your adult entertainment source... It's like *NetFlix*, but naked," Marvel says while mentioning the mandatory station identification and slogan.

"Marvel, you know that Tesla car models spell... SEXY? Pretty sure Teslas were made for swingers. I mean, there's a reason the cars are 'hands-free.' Elon Musk's favorite numbers are 69 and 420. He's a stoned horny dude," Seth adds.

"This Telsa orgy is going to put Teagan and Romulus from 'The MUSKeteers' way behind the rest of the pack and might cost them the race," Marvel says.

"So, who cares? It's the best part of the race so far. It looks like Romulus is getting behind, alright, behind a couple of different women. And if Big Willy doesn't stop jacking off, he'll also lose the race," Seth observes.

"Hey guys, are you getting all of this? It's a massive Telsa group sex party going on down there. Let's land and take a much closer look, for the viewers, of course. David, what the hell are you doing? Get the camera off me and back on the Tesla orgy. Fucking amateur," Candee Cane reports.

"Excellent, Candee Cane. Have fun. We will cut over to Tara, who has Scotty Braun from Mid-Life Crisis, for a quick interview while he fills up at the gas station," Marvel says.

"I'm buying a fucking Tesla," Seth quickly adds.

"Thank you, Marvel! No orgy happening at our location. I know this will be less thrilling for the audience, but I have last year's champion, Scotty Braun, in my presence. What are your thoughts about repeating as champions? Your teammate is miles behind you due to his excessive speeding ticket last night," Tara asks.

"I'm still feeling pretty good. I got off to a late start, and I had to take a massive dump because of my IBS," he replies, sharing too much information.

"Your bowel movements are not required knowledge for me or the audience. More importantly, who do you sense is the larger threat to dethroning you?" She follows up with another question.

"I'm not sure yet. Maybe the gay guys in the two Prius. That car can get some serious miles before refueling," he answers.

"One of them is a female. What about the speed and youth of team 'The Good Nine 11' in the Porsche?" She follows up.

"Really? One of them is a woman. Huh, who knew? No, I don't think they're a threat. They're too busy looking at themselves in the rearview mirror. Hey, what's the difference between a Porsche and a porcupine? Porcupines have pricks on the outside. How about this one? What is the definition of a lesbian? Another woman trying to do a man's job," Scotty says as he laughs at his own jokes.

Tara does not find his dad's jokes amusing and mutters, "I doubt they do a better job at it than me."

"Thank you for that quick interview, Tara. There doesn't appear to be any love lost between the Corvette and Porsche teams," Marvel says.

"Tara, you're correct; that was less thrilling. Now, can we go back to the Telsa fuck party?" Seth adds.

The two Karens from "The KarenVans" are getting a quick lunch at a Chick-fil-A in Macon, Georgia. They enter the restaurant, hoping to save time because the drive-thru line is long. This ends up being the wrong decision because their order takes even longer. Karen #2 becomes extremely impatient and annoyed and wants everyone in the restaurant to know.

"This is fucking ridiculous! How about you staff more people or cook faster? We shouldn't have to wait this long; it's chicken and fries, and it's not that hard! Do you even know who we are?" Karen #2 yells out at the teenage cashier.

"Holy shit, bro, that's the Karens from the NFX-33 race. I'm recording this shit and sending it to them. They'll pay good money for this," one of the male customers says to his friend as he pulls out his camera phone to record the event.

"Number 254, please, number 254!" One of the employees yells to the customer to pick up their order.

"254? What the actual fuck? My number is 236, and I'm still waiting! This is a conspiracy. Get me your manager right fucking now!" Karen #1 yells.

The number 254 customer grabs his food and looks at the Karens.

"Good luck!" he says with a smirk.

"Fuck you, asshole." Karen #1 says.

"Yes, ma'am, how can I assist you?" the manager says from behind the counter.

"How can you help me? Hmm, you can help me by giving me my fucking food before everyone that ordered after me gets theirs! Also, by staffing more people and getting a faster drive-thru, that's how you can help me, moron!" Karen #1 expresses herself.

"I'm sorry, ma'am; your order is coming up now," the manager says.

"It's about fucking time," She responds, snatching the to-go bag from his hands as they walk out of the restaurant.

The young man continues to record the incident and moves to the window as they walk back to their minivans.

Suddenly, one of the Karens starts throwing a massive fit in her vehicle. Both members of "The KarenVans" come storming back into the restaurant.

"What the fuck? I didn't get my waffle fries! Where are my waffle fries?" Karen #1 screams at the top of her voice.

"Waffle Fries! I want my waffle fries!" Karen #2 screams.

"And dipping sauce, don't forget my dipping sauce!" Karen #1 adds.

They start kicking over chairs and knocking napkin holders off of tables while just yelling. The manager quickly calls the police. Several people are recording this with their phones, but the young man has the best footage of the two Karens raging.

A few minutes later, the police arrive and arrest both Karens, who put up a fight, kicking and screaming, while resisting arrest.

"I did nothing wrong; I know my rights! This is America, and I have free speech. Fuck you, Chick-Fil-A. I'm going to Popeye's next time," Karen #1 yells as the police escort her out of the restaurant.

"The KarenVan's" race is over... and they never received their waffle fries and sauce.

Day 2 is coming to a close as the remaining contestants find a place to pull over and rest just before midnight. Marvel and Seth summarize the day's results to the "NFX-33" viewers.

"What a day Seth! We lost a few teams early in the day. The Karens are cooling off in a Macon, Georgia, jail cell for their 'waffle fries' outburst. Thank you for the great footage sent to us by Jeff Mayhew and the numerous hilarious memes that came from it," Marvel reports.

"Crazy day, Marvel; we got a report about an hour ago from Candee Cane that the Telsa group has started a 'Love Community' just outside Gainesville, Florida. They're calling themselves 'The Branch Elonians.' Apparently, Big Willy from 'The Whitey Fords' has traded his truck in for a Telsa, turned Democrat, and decided to join them," Seth adds.

"Those sex cults are hard to resist. Sid and I used to be in one back in the mid-90s for about four months. He convinced me to leave a week before they all died in a freak accident. During a pool sex party, their giant electric neon Flamingo fell into the pool and electrocuted all of them," Marvel reveals.

"I learn something new and amazing about you every day, Marvel. Anyway, the second member of 'Whitey Fords,' Andrew Wright, was arrested with a bunch of anti-vaxxers storming the Georgia capital building demanding 'no more masks or mandatory shots,' even though Covid-19 has been a dead issue for years now. Those Trumpsters just can't let things go," Seth adds.

"White pick-up truck drivers are Trump-supporting anti-vaxxers? No way, who would have thought? Any last thoughts before we sign off for the night, Seth?" Marvel asks.

"What did the janitor say when he jumped out of the closet?... Supplies! Why couldn't the bicycle stand up by itself?... It was two tired," Seth jokes.

"Okay, I see that Scotty Braun from 'Mid-Life Crisis' has rubbed off on you. Good night, everyone. See you tomorrow morning for more race coverage," Marvel adds.

Saturday morning begins day 3 of "The NFX-33" race. The end credits of Sid's sixth and highest-grossing porn film, "Pirates of Cari's Bean: At World's Rear End," where Sid stars as *Captain Jackov Morrow*, are concluding. The viewers who weren't already beating their meat to Sid's swashbuckling adventure are tuning in for today's race coverage. The teams are spread out over the middle of the country, and most are more than halfway to the finish line. The current leader is Gustavo Green, on the team "Wokeswagen," driving the Volkswagen Jetta. He pulls into a gas station just outside of Omaha, Nebraska, to fuel up and start the day's journey. His next closest rivals are Brad and Chad Esquire, who are on "The Good Nine 11" team in Kansas City, Kansas. The Esquires decide to travel on I-70 towards Denver, Colorado.

The "NFX-33" broadcast starts with Marvel and Seth providing the live updates. Marvel is bright-eyed, bushy-tailed, and ready to go. Seth still wears sunglasses and looks like he had a long, wild night.

"Here we go, Seth, the start of Day 3. It appears that Gustavo Green from Team Wokeswagen is our current leader. The Porche driving douchebags are in 2nd place and chose a different route. This could be an exciting finish with only seven teams remaining in the race," Marvel starts the broadcast.

"Yeah, should be close," Seth replies while yawning.

"Damn, Seth, riveting reply. Are you okay, buddy? I know you're not a morning person, but you look half-dead," Marvel asks.

"Sorry, Marvel, it's late night. I did some standup at the Comedy Store and then went out for drinks with my comedian friend Teina Manu. I'm on about two hours of sleep right now," Seth explains.

"Oh man, well, you're in for a long day buddy. Maybe you can nap later, and I'll handle the broadcasting duties with Tara and Candee Cane," Marvel offers.

"It's all good. I hear Gustavo Green owns a mushroom-growing company called *Fun Gus*. I didn't think that would be legal, and I need to speak to him after the race," Seth says.

"Not those kinds of mushrooms, Seth. He grows legal mushrooms for supplements and health benefits, not psychedelics. Besides, shrooms are the last thing you need right now," Marvel laughs.

"Mushrooms for health reasons? That's silly. Just throw them on my pizza. Let's go to the lovely Ashlee "Candee Cane" Sundberg for our first interview and update today," Seth says.

Candee Cane and cameraman David stand beside Gaylord Edwards from the Rainbow Power team at a charging station in Nashville, Tennessee.

"Fungus doesn't belong on pizza, Seth," David responds.

"David, shut the hell up! Me point camera, Me no speak, you fucking Neanderthal," she says using a caveman's voice.

"Sorry about that, Seth. I'm here with Gaylord from the Rainbow Power team. He's preparing for day 3 of the race. Gaylord, you're behind right now and not in the good way you're accustomed to. What is your plan to catch up to the leaders?" she asks.

"Yeah, we lost some time here in Nashville. Gaylene and I heard about a gay bar from our friends, Dave and Felipe, called Peckers. So, naturally, we had to check that out. Honey, we're not worried about the leaders; we'll catch up today," Gaylord answers.

"Peckers? That sounds like fun! I stayed here last night, just me and BOB. So, where was my invite?" Candee Cane jokes... kind of.

"Bob? Is that your camera guy?" he asks.

"Oh no, my camera guy is David, and he's taken a vow of celibacy for some new religion he joined. He's a freak! BOB is my Battery-Operated-Boyfriend," Candee Cane explains while laughing.

"Oh, sugar, I'm sorry! We'll take you next time for sure. Besides, I've seen you with Sid in 'Thighway to Hell', so I know you can rock a cock and swim in trim," Gaylord replies.

"Ahh, you're so sweet. I still would have gone because the batteries on my BOB ran out. Speaking of Gaylene, where is your teammate now?" Candee Cane asks.

"That bitch is in the hotel room with a couple of ladies she met last night. I have to ensure she's awake and on the road," he answers.

"Hmm, a couple of ladies. What room is she in? I'll go check on her for you. David, stay here," Candee Cane concludes the interview.

"Great job, Candee Cane; let's quickly cut over to Tara while she has Gustavo Green still outside his car," Marvel interrupts.

A few miles outside of Omaha, Nebraska, Gustavo Green is finishing up filling his gas tank. The drivers aren't always aware of the location of many other drivers, except from what they hear from fans, reports on the internet, or updates from the "NFX-33" broadcasting crew. Tara "Minxy" Anders and cameraman Jake catch up to him before he leaves and reveal some breaking news to the viewers about his teammate, of which he was unaware.

"Good morning, Gustavo. I won't keep you long. What are you feeling after discovering your teammate Skyline Mason's situation?" Tara asks.

"Situation? I'm afraid I don't know what you speak of. Please tell me what you know," he needs clarification.

"Oh, I assumed you would have been the first to know. Once again, my superior investigating skills out-pace the media. Skyline Mason was arrested this morning around 5:00 a.m. at a scheduled slaughterhouse protest rally. I'm afraid she is out of the race," she informs.

"Fuck, that's why she didn't answer her phone this morning. Well, good for her. Someone needs to stand up to those butchering murderers of poor, innocent animals. That's why we only eat plant-based foods, like my mushrooms from 'Fun Gus' products," Gustavo replies as he climbs back into his car to leave.

"Thank you, Gustavo, and good luck on the rest of your journey in the NFX-33. I recall when Sid and I indulged in a bag of mushroom narcotics while filming his eleventh film and, tragically, my last, "Big Trousers in Little Jhina." That was an exquisite time. Back to you, gentlemen, in the studio," Tara says.

"Excellent reporting, Minxy. It's tough news about Skyline Mason, but her protesting won't stop me from getting my favorite double bacon cheeseburger from *Hodads* in San Diego. I drive down there once a month for that delicious pound of meat," Seth rambles.

"I'm hungry now. Send the intern out to get us some cheeseburgers from *Burger She Wrote*. Screw that meat-protesting crap; I could eat a juicy burger right now," Marvel adds.

"Just one problem, Seth. It's too early. They're not open yet. Send him to get some breakfast from *Mel's drive-in* on Sunset instead. Come take our orders, intern," Seth says.

The intern walks to the broadcasting desk with paper and pencil to write their orders.

"How rude of us just barking commands at the intern; I'm sure you have a name. What is it?" Marvel says, realizing they sound like celebrity dickheads.

"It's Intern, sir. Intern Ramirez. My parents were new to the country, and the doctors told them it was an important name in Hollywood as a joke. They didn't know any better," he answers.

Seth and Marvel look at each other for a few seconds and then start cracking up. Intern Ramirez isn't affected by the laughter; he's used to it. He takes their orders and leaves to get them the requested breakfast.

Midnight is approaching day 3 of the race, and the competitors must plan where to stop for the mandatory rest time. The day was action-packed and full of surprises that the *NetFux* crew is preparing to recap at the end of the day three broadcast. Candee Cane is ready to provide one last interview of the day with Lori "Eyes" Bellinger and Christian Hartling of "Jeepers Creepers" at another Denny's in Bozeman, Montana. The countless dachshunds in her Jeep are barking at the sexy reporter and her cameraman.

"David, leave the fucking dogs alone and focus. Lori, you guys are among the race's leaders, and it will come down to the finish tomorrow. It's impressive that you both are still traveling together. Was this your strategy from the start? Also, the viewers want to know, are you a couple?" Candee Cane asks.

"Jeep, Jeep, Jeep. Jeeping Jeep Jeep. Jeep Jeep. And Fuck No!" Lori responds while Christian ignores the question and waves at every passing vehicle on the road.

"Well, I'll just assume that was your plan because I have no fucking clue what you just said. Except for the 'Fuck No' part, which I'm assuming was to the last question. Back to you guys in the studio. There's no point in asking another question. One only says 'Jeep,' and the other plays 'Captain Friendly' to everyone driving by. Oh, that sounds like a porn character, 'Captain Friendly'. *Permission to cum aboard, Captain,*" Candee Cane replies with a seductive ending.

"Thank you, Candee; I'm surprised those two are still together, let alone in the lead. Let's cut over to Tara for her last interview of the night," Marvel says.

"That Jeep chick could be the next Disney movie, '101 dachshunds.' Except she'll have to be re-casted with a black actress," Seth quips.

Tara and Jake are standing at the entrance to the lobby of a Holiday Inn Express with the two brothers, Brad and Chad Esquire, of the team "The Good Nine 11", driving in Porsche 911s.

"Thank you, Marvel. I'm catching up with Brad and Chad Esquire before they enjoy a good night's slumber here in beautiful Ogden, Utah. What was your bold strategy to take this route when all the other competitors decided to travel on the 90 north of your location?" Tara asks.

"Unlike the other drivers, we did some research before the race began, and we found out that there are fewer highway patrol officers and less traffic on the 84. We're more prepared and intelligent," Brad, the oldest brother, replies.

"I understand. However, you are currently 92 minutes behind the race leaders in Bozeman, Montana. What is your strategy for gaining ground?" Tara follows up.

"First, we'll get a good night's sleep in a comfortable bed instead of sleeping in our cars, like those peasants do. You're welcome to join us again, Minxy. Then, we will increase our speed tomorrow with fewer chances of highway patrol cars. Last, since the other teams need to learn how to research, they're ignorant that just outside of Spokane, Washington, the highway is down to one lane for almost 10 miles due to construction. That tactical error will allow us to pass them for the lead and easily win," Chad answers confidently.

"Impressive. It sounds to me like you young men have it all figured out. Thank you for the invite this evening, but I will pass this time. I wish you luck with the rest of the NFX-33," Tara says, finishing the interview.

"You're welcome. Last night was truly a blessing and privilege for you. My brother and I are always more than willing to rock your world again," Brad responds.

"Well, Sugar, I can assure you that last night it wasn't my world that got rocked," Minxy replies in disappointment.

"Those are some confident and lucky brothers right there, Seth," Marvel says.

"I'm not a narcissistic spoiled douchebag, but I did stay at a Holiday Inn Express," Seth jokes, mocking the hotel chain's old commercial campaigns.

"Okay, Seth, the station is about to cut to Sid's first film, the one that started it all... Missionary Possible, in which he plays super spy *Eathem Kuntz*," Marvel says.

"I would have to say that his sequel and seventh film, 'Missionary Possible: Rogue Sensation' is his best work. And he does his own stunts and his own fucking, of course," Seth adds.

"That one's on right after. The network is playing the films back-to-back tonight," Marvel reveals.

"Well, shit, I guess I'm not getting any sleep. See you in the morning for the final day, Marvel." Seth ends the broadcast, and the opening credits for "Missionary Possible" begin.

The morning of the final day of the race has arrived. The remaining drivers are in the same time zone and will leave simultaneously. The clock reads 5:51 a.m. Mountain Standard Time. The drivers start getting into their vehicles and preparing for the race.

NetFux begins the morning's broadcast with some breaking news from Tara. They immediately cut to her at a campsite where team "Wokeswagens" pack their tents and camping supplies.

"Good morning, Marvel, Seth, and all the *NetFux* viewers. Team "Wokeswagens" has announced they will withdraw from the NFX-33. Instead, they will travel to the capitol in Helena for an organized march against the producers, actors, and crew members of the wildly hit TV show, 'Yellowstone.' I have Skyline Mason with me now to answer my riveting, important questions. Why are you quitting on a chance at one million dollars to protest a popular television show?" Tara asks.

"We don't see it as quitting or as the show is a hit; to us, it's our civic duty to improve this country. We can do better!" Skyline states.

"I can feel the passion in your voice. However, why specifically this TV show and not several more filming in nearby areas?" Tara digs.

"We both felt that the damage the show is doing to Montana's beautiful landscape and natural resources is far more costly than a million dollars. We must fight to keep this gorgeous land intact instead of becoming a major Hollywood studio with a theme park with rides, churros, and character-costumed performers," Skyline replies.

"That might seem a bit far-fetched to our viewers. I'm sure the production team is cautious about filming a hit TV show in a beautiful protected land. What do I know? I've only won 2 late-night Emmys, 5 AVN awards, and 1 Pulitzer Prize for my best-selling auto-biography, 'From Teensy to Minxy'!" Tara says.

"Okay! We have one less team to worry about on the last day of the 'NFX-33." Marvel adds.

"Rip and Kayce would take those woke protesting fucks to the 'Train Station,'" Seth says, referencing the TV show "Yellowstone."

The remaining drivers are approaching Seattle, and it will be a close finish. The *NetFux* helicopters are flying above some leaders to capture the finish. Tara and Candee Cane are at the finish line, waiting to interview the winners and losers. The stage where Sid will present the trophy and million-dollar checks is empty.

"Cut to Chopper 1; it appears the leaders, "Jeepers Creepers," are suddenly pulling into a mall area. Now is not a great time to go shoe shopping," Seth reports.

Lori "Eyes" Bellinger and Christian Hartling are parking the jeeps in a crowded shopping mall in Seattle. Lori gets out with a bag full of different plastic rubber duckies. She starts walking around the parking lot, placing them on other Jeeps. Christian is helping but mostly waving at people driving by.

"I can't believe this; they stopped to go 'ducking' right before the finish line," Marvel reports.

"What the fuck is 'ducking'? Is this another weird click thing with Jeep owners, like the special wave they have for each other?" Seth asks.

"You're supposed to show love to other Jeep owners by leaving them a rubber duckie on their windshield. They call it 'ducking'. They couldn't resist the number of Jeeps in that parking lot. Well, they're done," Marvel reports.

"Well, probably because it is a Jeep dealership," Seth says.

"Seth, we must cut to Chopper 2 for a huge update. It appears that 'The British Invasion' is stuck trying to figure out the round-a-bout and is driving around in circles. They've lost the lead to 'Rainbow Alphabet' and 'The Good Nine 11'," Marvel adds.

"I think it's down to two teams, Marvel. The gays and the douchebags. I have to say I'm cheering for the gays on this one," Seth admits.

"Dale Earnhardt is turning over in this grave," Seth agrees.

The final two drivers are neck and neck, nearly a mile from *Lumen Field* and the finish line. The leaders, Brad from "The Good Nine 11" and Gaylene from "Rainbow Alphabet," look at each other briefly to size each other up. They are closing in on the entry to *Lumen Field*'s parking lot, and the finish line is in sight. Thousands of cheering and screaming fans are lining the streets; both *NetFux* helicopters are flying above, and Sid is walking up the stage steps to view the finish line only a few yards before him.

Suddenly, about two blocks ahead, Scotty Braun's Corvette of the team "Mid-life Crisis" comes whipping around a corner to take the lead. He starts throwing out banana peels while laughing hysterically, pretending to be in the video game *Mario Cart*. Brad drives straight over them, while Gaylene, believing that her car will spin into a 360-degree frenzy like the game, tries to avoid them, causing her to fall into third place.

The two sports cars are almost side by side, with Scotty just ½ car lengths ahead. Brad accelerates and is inching closer to the lead. Scotty looks to his right and sees Brad staring at him with a smile as if he has a secret.

Scotty points over to the side of the road so that Brad can look at something. He turns his gaze from Scotty to the Abercrombie & Fitch store window displaying "Labor Day 50% off" signs. Brad slows down to park but realizes it was a ploy to distract him. He presses down on the gas pedal and jets forward in Scotty's direction.

"This is it, the final 20 yards, and Brad or Chad—I can't tell them apart—is closing in on the leader, Scotty Braun," Marvel reports.

"Brad's the one who keeps looking at himself in the rearview mirror; see, he just did it again," Seth explains.

Brad's Porsche needed to be a little faster to catch up with the 2024 red Corvette and Scotty Braun. He crossed the finish line and won the race. He and his teammate, Keith Michaels, repeat as champions and win another $1,000,000 each. Gaylene came across the finish line a few seconds after Brad to complete the top three.

The remaining drivers all finish within the next hour to conclude the race. The final results are displayed on the television screen:

Winner- Scotty Braun "Mid-life Crisis" Corvette
2nd place- Brad Esquire III "The Good Nine 11" Porsche
3rd place- Gaylene Garcia "Rainbow Alphabet" Prius
4th place- Gaylord Edwards "Rainbow Alphabet" Prius
5th Place- Chad Esquire "The Good Nine 11" Porsche
6th Place- Thomas Harris "British Invasion" Mini Cooper
7th Place- Liam Jones "British Invasion" Mini Cooper
8th Place- Lori "Eyes" Bellinger "Jeepers Creepers" Jeep
9th Place- Christian Hartling "Jeepers Creepers" Jeep
10th Place- Keith Michaels "Mid-life Crisis" Corvette

Sid approaches the microphone on the stage. The drivers are standing on the ground before him, and the fans are cheering and going crazy. Sid quiets them down with one wave and looks down at the drivers. He gives them an enthusiastic thumbs up because he knows that the "NFX-33" viewership of the race was over 25% higher than last year, and more prominent sponsors will be calling to advertise during next year's race. He gave a congratulations speech and called the winners, Scotty Braun and Keith Michaels, to the stage. Sid hands them their checks and trophies. The crowd goes wild again for the victors, and Sid fades to the back of the stage and disappears behind a "NetFux 3300" backdrop. Tara and Candee Cane approach the winners for an interview.

"Hey, gentlemen, how does it feel to successfully defend your championship title and win the NFX-33 for two straight years?" Tara asks with excitement.

"There's nothing like Detroit Muscle power. Viva La Corvette. That reminds me of a joke: what's the only thing that grows in Detroit? The crime rates," Scotty answers the questions with follow-up dad joke humor.

"Actually, Corvettes are manufactured in Bowling Green, Kentucky," Tara follows up.

"What are you going to do with new winnings? I'm free tonight," Candee Cane says jokingly... kind of.

"Sorry, Candee Cane, I'm a happily married man. I'm going to take my family out to dinner at *Applebee*'s. That's where we go for all special occasions," Scotty answers.

"Thank you so much, team 'Mid-Life Crisis,' and congratulations on your magnificent victory. Back the gentlemen in the studio. It was a pleasure as always," Tara says, cutting off Keith Michael's chance to answer the question.

"Well, Seth, that concludes this year's 'NetFux 3300'. What a great race, full of twists and turns, literally," Marvel says.

"Yeah, but Applebee's? Come on, bro, take your family to somewhere better than that place... Like Chili's," Seth recommends.

"Hey, be happy. He could've said 'Chick-fil-A'. I hear they have waffle fries and sauce," Marvel jokes, and they both laugh.

"Oh shit, we have some breaking news, Marvel. It seems we forgot all about 'The Streetful Dead.' You remember them, the stoners driving the Volkswagen Buses? It appears they're still in the parking lot of *Hard Rock Stadium* in Miami. They got stoned and never left," Seth reports.

"Hey, the *RIFF* music festival is coming to *Hard Rock Stadium* next weekend; they should just probably stay there for that," Marvel adds.

"Marvel, it was great working with you again, my friend. I can't wait until next Sunday when we get to cover *Majestic's* inaugural NFL broadcast in Miami," Seth concludes his broadcast.

"Indeed, Seth, I'm excited to move over to Sid's other streaming service, *Majestic*, for some pro football action. This is Marvel and Seth signing off. It was a pleasure to provide coverage of this year's 'NetFux 3300' to all the viewers. Now, stay tuned for Sid's tenth and most controversial film, 'Skindler's Fist,' here on *NetFux*," Marvel ends the broadcast.

"I just watched him and Minxy in his third film, Pirates of Cari's Bean: Dead Men Get No Tail,' probably my favorite of his eleven films," Seth adds before the broadcast cuts out.

REVERSE THE CURSE

The Miami Dolphins will start to defend their AFC championship title this Sunday night against the New York Jets. The Dolphins are one of the favorites to win it all this year, even after last year's heartbreaking Superbowl loss to the Detroit Lions. The Dolphin's current run of back-to-back Superbowls the past two seasons, winning the Lombardi Trophy two years ago, was mainly due to their stellar defense, star quarterback Blake Powers they drafted with the 2nd pick from the University of Michigan three years ago, and the 7-year veteran tight end Trevor Kacey.

You've been living in a cave if you have yet to hear of Blake and Trevor by now. Their star power grows yearly with the number of commercials we see them in. I bet you can't watch TV for one hour without seeing at least one of their faces promoting some product, fast food place, or insurance company. The ones they do together for the "City Field" insurance company are the most annoying, and it seems like it's aired every 15 minutes on all sports networks. They're always accompanied by the more annoying reoccurring character, "Drake from City Field." I guess winning the Superbowl and having a great agent allows you these perks... The spoils of success.

During last year's bye week, Trevor Kacey met mega pop star diva Taylor Quick at a Miami beach club party for mutual friend and Hollywood "A-lister" actor Preston Harding. Taylor and Preston had a brief fling during her marriage, but nothing romantically became of it, just friends. Taylor and Trevor hit it off immediately, but they took a few weeks before making it publicly official. Taylor was coming off her divorce last year from Samir Nazari, a wealthy businessman from the Phoenix area. She met and married him when she was in her "I want to meet a regular guy and not a celebrity" phase. Taylor got bored with him after a year of marriage. Now that she's back to dating someone famous, she can focus on joining the elite EPCC (Entertainment Power Couples Club). A particular club only reserved for married power couples in the entertainment and sports industry that was created by Beyonce and Jay Z ten years ago. Rumor is that the EPCC influences entertainment and sports labor negotiations, casting, Super Bowl half-time shows, celebrity match-making, and many more pop culture trends.

Trevor and Taylor, better known by their nickname TayTrev, which was given to them by the public (or by the EPCC, as conspiracy theorists would have you believe), have been dominating the tabloids. They've appeared on numerous television networks over the past several months. Roberto Tyler, a member of the Paparazzi, first captured their surprise romance that came out of nowhere. Roberto got photos of TayTrev holding hands on the beach and sharing a kiss during dinner while in Miami. Roberto used a wetsuit and waterproof camera to capture the beach photo, seen worldwide. Roberto could retire for the money he was paid for that revealing photo. He captured the couple's secret in one shot, and the photo forced them to acknowledge their relationship with the world, which they didn't want to do until after football season.

They made their relationship official when Taylor was spotted in a luxury suite at *Hard Rock Stadium* during the last three weeks of last year's season, and the beach photo was released. The Dolphins finished 12-5, losing those last three games that Taylor attended. They barely won their two playoff games that Taylor couldn't attend, followed by the historic loss to the Detroit Lions in the Super Bowl, in which Taylor Quick was the half-time show entertainment. Miami was favored to win, but the Lions were victorious in their first Super Bowl ever. Since that time, the TayTrev story has monopolized the headlines. *Could this be the new "America's Couple"?*

Miami Dolphins fans are split in their feelings about TayTrev. Half the fans think it's sweet and are happy that Trevor and Taylor have this young romance. The other half believes she's a curse to the team and Kacey. The team has performed poorly since her appearance.

Of course, the fans of all other teams hate it, and they're sick of hearing about TayTrev. They've had enough of seeing her mug on the TV screen every time Kacey catches the ball, which some fans will point out hasn't happened as much since the diva's invasion into Trevor's heart.

The start of the new season for both teams is about to begin. The Dolphins and Jets are preparing for the opening kickoff. The fans are going wild for the return of their Super Bowl champs from 2 years ago and the runner-up last year. The streaming giant *Majestic*, the non-pornographic network owned by billionaire Sid Sanderson, is covering the game and will have a camera fixated on Taylor's luxury suite for the whole game to capture her reactions. *That is precisely what all football-loving fans want to see after every great play.*

"Here we go, Seth, the start of an amazing football season on *Majestic's* inaugural season coverage of the NFL. Will the Dolphins return to the Super Bowl for a third consecutive year, or can teams stop them? How exciting is this?" says Marvel Spencer, lead sportscaster for Sunday Night Football.

"So exciting. I won't need that little blue pill tonight, Marvel; I'm already hard," Seth replies.

"Seth, please remember this isn't like our coverage of the 'NFX-3300' on *NetFux*. We have to be a little more careful in what we say," Marvel reminds Seth that they're on a more family-friendly network now.

"Oh shit, my bad. I'm looking forward to Sunday nights in the broadcast booth with you, Marvel. Mr. Sanderson thought we did a good enough job covering the 'NFX-3300' this year that he gave us this gig, too," Seth says.

"Exactly, Seth. We have some familiar faces from *NetFux* who helped cover last week's big race. The always beautiful Tara 'Minxy' Anders is reporting from the Miami sidelines, and the sultry vixen known as Ashlee 'Candee Cane' Sunberg will be walking the Jets sidelines. Let's go to Minxy now," Marvel introduces the two ladies.

"Hey, Marvel and Seth, so good to be working with you again after last weekend's exciting cross-country race. I spoke with Miami's Trevor Kacey a few minutes ago and asked him if this extra attention dating Taylor Quick caused any distractions or lack of focus by him or the team. He responded that he and the team are more focused than last year. Since this was my first time seeing Trevor Kacey up close and in person, I understood why Taylor wanted a piece of that hunk of a man. Over to you, Candee Cane," Minxy reports.

Candee Cane emerges from the blue medical tent on the sideline, wiping her mouth and straightening her tight blouse and leather skirt.

"Sorry, guys. I got a quick word from New York Jets running back DeMarcus Willis while he got his ankle looked at before game time. He feels his ankle, which he twisted in pre-season, is good to go," Candee Cane says.

"Yeah, Candee Cane, you had an in-depth and intimate one-on-one interview with DeMarcus. One could say it was an exclusive and explosive report. You missed a spot on your blouse, Lewinsky." Seth mocks.

"Thank you, ladies, for those important notes to the game. As always, your sideline reporting is top-notch. Seth, I think Miami should dominate with Blake and Trevor going 100%," Marvel says.

"Sorry, Marvel, but I'm sick of seeing those perfect men's faces. They're fucking everywhere. The pair of them are on every damn commercial, either together or separately," Seth complains.

"Here we go, Seth. The kickoff is happening now with a touchback for the Miami Dolphins. This will be a great division rivalry matchup," Marvel says.

"Nah, the Jets suck, and Miami is an elite team. This will be a blowout by the Dolphins," Seth confidently shares.

The game ends, and the results aren't what the experts, most fans, Seth, and some players expected.

"Well, that sucked; Miami lost 38-7 to the crappy New York Jets on the day they raised the AFC Championship banner for the fans. Not a great way to start the new season for the champs," Seth says after the end of the game.

"Yeah, many fans left by the end of the 3rd quarter. Trevor only caught one pass for negative yardage. It's probably not what Taylor Quick had in mind," Marvel reports.

"I'm pretty sure it's not what our network *Majestic* had in mind, either. They were hoping for more Taylor photo ops when Kacey touched the ball. Hey Marvel, when Taylor Quick walks on the beach, does she become Quick Sand?" Seth says, laughing proudly at this dad joke he just made up.

"Nice one, Seth. Okay, America, we will see you in the Motor City next Sunday as the Super Bowl champion Detroit Lions take on the Vikings," Marvel signs off.

"I still can't get over hearing 'Super Bowl champion Detroit Lions.' That is crazy. They were bad for so so so long. Detroit will crush the poor Vikings, who some say will lose all 17 games this season. Hey Seth, What is the difference between the Vikings and a dollar bill? You can still get four quarters out of a dollar bill," Seth comments and jokes.

The NFL season is approaching its five-week mark, and the defending AFC champs have a 1-4 record. Their only win was against the Green Bay Packers last week, and it just so happens to be the only game Taylor Quick hasn't attended this season. She was busy performing a concert filmed for Disney Plus in Los Angeles. The fans opposing the TayTrev romance have added that fact to their claim that... Taylor Quick is a jinx.

Some Dolphin fans have started a petition to ban her from games. Many of them continue to reach out to Kacey's social media accounts, begging him to "dump that bitch" and restore the winning. Since the existence of TayTrev, the Dolphins are 1-9 at the games she's attended and 3-0 at games she wasn't there.

Their next game is a Super Bowl rematch with the Detroit Lions in Miami on Sunday Night Football on *Majestic*. The Detroit fans travel well, and there will undoubtedly be a massive "Honolulu Blue Wave" fan presence. The Lions are favored by ten and are running on all cylinders with a 4-1 record... Taylor is expected to attend.

"Welcome to Miami, football fans. We have an epic matchup between last year's Super Bowl teams. Can Dolphins get revenge, or will the Lions remain supreme over the sea mammals? We're about to find out. Where land and sea collide,

The Lions vs. Dolphins coming up next on *Majestic*," Marvel reports.

"Well, I see Taylor's in her usual spot. So, that's a no. The Dolphins will not get their revenge. Detroit by ten easily," Seth remarks.

"Seth, you know you're supposed to remain impartial and just call the game? Not give your opinion about who will win," Marvel says while chuckling.

"Fuck that, fans want to hear the truth. Everyone knows it, but they're too scared to upset Taylor's fans, 'The Quickies.' The Dolphins suck since she has started dating Kacey," Seth implies.

"Yes, they played badly during that time and when she attended the game. However, I feel it's just the NFL. Since Miami is at the top, every team will give them their best. They'll weather the storm," Marvel replies.

"Detroit's Jeremy Groff, who played a brilliant game, takes his knee to run out the clock and give the Lions their 5th win of the season. The Dolphins will fall to 1-5 after this crushing loss. Detroit 34 Miami 13," Marvel reports the final results of today's game.

"The Dolphins look more like Guppies out there. They're outmatched and outplayed. Detroit looks like those man-eating animals of last season, and I believe they will win another Super Bowl. Perhaps we have a dynasty in Detroit," Seth says.

"Dynasty in Detroit? Seth, you're getting a lot better at journalism. You might not need to do stand-up anymore," Marvel compliments Seth.

"Maybe so, but Taylor had better be careful when leaving the stadium. The fins fans look restless. They're throwing beer, food, and anything else they can get their hands on at the window to her suite. Security is no match for this riled-up bunch. The jinx conspiracy is growing with every loss," Seth adds.

The *Majestic* cameras capture the fans' uproar as they pelt the glass window that just recently had Taylor Quick peering out of. The fans don't realize she's been gone since the end of the 3rd quarter. Security is just trying to escort everyone out of the section and stadium. Finally, after a couple of minutes, they settle down and start to chant, "Go home, Taylor! Go home, Taylor!"

The players are quiet, reflecting on the loss, undressing their dirty uniforms and the usual after-game routines of an NFL locker room. Blake Powers stands up and addresses Trevor Kacey, his teammate and best friend.

"Hey bro, how attached are you to Taylor?" he asks.

This upsets Trevor, and he comes running after him. A few players get between them to prevent a locker-room fight. Blake isn't alone in his thoughts.

"Yeah, dump that bitch. She's fucking jinxing us," a player yells from the back of the locker room.

"Fuck all of you. I love her!" Trevor declares.

The whole team, in unison, gives out a big loud... "Aww!"

"Bro, imagine if you dump her now. She'll write a hit song about you. So, you can tell your family that song is about me for the rest of your life. That's pretty cool," Blake suggests.

There's a few seconds of silence, and the locker room laughs, including Trevor. The brotherhood of an NFL team trumps a celebrity romance every time.

The following week, the Miami Dolphins lost again on the road to the Buffalo Bills and now have the worst record in the league at 1-6. The fans have completely turned on them and are calling for Trevor Kacey to dump Taylor Quick or trade him. They've even united as one and started to ban going to games.

Only 10,000 fans attended next week's home game against the New England Patriots. Most were Patriots fans and a few Dolphin fans who don't support the Taylor Quick jinx theory. Taylor Quick would not attend this matchup due to a prior commitment to a new music video shoot. The Dolphins beat the first-place Patriots 17-14 for their 2nd win. Trevor had 8 catches for 83 yards and a touchdown, his best game of the season.

The win would fuel the fire of what is now being called "A Quick Problem" by fans and local media. The players, front office, and fans all feel the strain of this alleged jinx the superstar diva and all-pro tight end have caused by their whirlwind romance. He is head-over-heels for Taylor and is blinded by what nearly everyone says.

The Dolphins' owner, billionaire Steven Gross, has called an emergency meeting for Monday morning after their win against New England. In attendance are head coach Mike McDonald, offensive coordinator and former NFL quarterback Jim Douglas, and general manager Ahmed Bashar. The men sit around a large oval conference table at the Miami Dolphins' headquarters.

"Gentlemen, Ahmed and I have been secretly shopping Kacey around the league for trade value and options before today's trade deadline. Not a single team still in playoff contention, 75% of the league, will touch him with a 10-foot crossbar. The only team interested in trading for him is the Chicago Bears, who feel the jinx can't do much worse for their season. They're willing to give us next year's number 1 pick, which at this time is the 3rd pick overall and a 2nd round pick the year after," Owner Steven Gross informs the group.

"Mr. Gross, you've been shopping one of our star players behind our backs? That doesn't sit well with me," Head Coach Mike McDonald says annoyedly.

"Well, Mike, being the worst team in the league doesn't sit well with me. Kacey isn't going to end his relationship with Taylor, and we're losing fans daily. In one way or another, the jinx is real," Steven Gross replies.

"Come on, we don't all believe in this superstitious bullshit. She's lovely, and Trevor is madly in love with her. We just need to get out of this slump, and it's not jinx!" OC Jim Douglas adds.

"Sorry, gentlemen. We might have to pull the trigger on this one. I'm calling Chicago at 3:30 pm today before the 4 pm deadline and accepting the trade unless something better comes along," GM Ahmed Bashar says.

"This isn't right!" Mike McDonald shouts as he storms out of the conference room, followed by Jim Douglas.

Later that day, just a few hours before the NFL trade deadline, the entertainment tabloid giant TMZ reports some breaking news from Los Angeles.

"This is just in from our freelance photographer, Roberto Tyler. We have the exclusive video footage of Taylor Quick and rapper and country music star Cunway East engaged in a passionate kiss after shooting their duet music video over this past weekend," The TMZ Reporter informs.

"So, while Kacey was finally scoring in Miami, Taylor was also scoring in Los Angeles," Another TMZ Member quips.

The TMZ Newsroom is filled with cast members laughing as they continue to report and show the kiss repeatedly on air.

A small statue of the soon-to-be Hall of Fame tight end Rob Gronkowski soars across the room and strikes the 70-inch Samsung smart TV hanging on the wall of Trevor Kacey's home. The TV screen cracks but doesn't completely break, still showing Taylor's tongue down Cunway East's throat.

"Bro, fuck her, at least now you know. Since losing, our media coverage has been dropping and becoming more negative. Her PR people probably told her your relationship was toxic now and to move on. You know how those Hollywood celebrities roll," Blake Powers says while sitting on Trevor's couch.

"I can't believe this fucking bitch. I told her I loved her for the first time just before she left. I should have known once she replied, 'You're the best, Trevor' and not 'I love you too.' What an idiot!" Trevor says.

"Nah, bro, just blinded by a hot piece of celebrity ass. I call it Star-Fucked; lots of bitches suffer from it around me. Think of it this way: the fans will start loving you again. You can get any hot piece of ass you want right here in Miami, and trust me, there's a lot of it. Plus, maybe we'll start winning some games," Blake says.

"Oh fuck, that reminds me, the coach called like an hour ago and said they're going to trade me to Chicago today before the deadline since I won't break up with Taylor. I need to call him right now because I'm finished with that cheating whore.

And seriously, bro, she hooks up with that ugly country-rapping freaky-looking dude? I wouldn't take her back just from pride alone," Trevor says while grabbing his cell phone.

"Yeah, who the fuck decided to mix country and rap as a music genre? Watch bro, somebody like Beyonce will do a country album next. And what kind of name is Cunway East? I blame this shit on Nashville. That's why I hate going there to play the Titans, all the fucking artistic weirdos there. It's the Austin, Texas of the Midwest," Blake agrees while Trevor frantically calls his coach.

"Dammit, he isn't answering. Neither is Jim. I don't want to play for the shitting Bears, bro. Go from Miami to Chi-raq, screw that," Trevor complains.

"Let's go. We have enough time to drive to headquarters and catch Ahmed before he completes the deal. I'll drive!" Blake commands as he grabs his phone, keys, and sunglasses.

"Yeah, I'll keep calling and texting them while you drive. I'll also text that whore that we're finished, and she can't fuck that Cunty East dude all she wants. He's probably got Peyronie disease, that carrot dick, mother fucker," Trevor continues to complain about his newly discovered romantic tsunami.

The two teammates and best friends race out of the large home and into Blake's red *Maserati MC20*. He speeds out of the driveway and down the road. The headquarters is about 30 minutes away, and the NFL deadline is in 90 minutes, which means they have 60 minutes left when they arrive at Dolphin's headquarters before Ahmed calls the Chicago Bears general manager to finalize the blockbuster trade and complete Trevor's worst nightmare... Becoming a Chicago Bear.

Blake is traveling over 100 MPH down the Florida Turnpike toward the stadium and headquarters, weaving in and out of traffic like a scene from Fast and the Furious. They're both willing to risk their lives to stop Kacey from becoming a Chicago Bear. To be fair, most NFL players would probably do the same.

"Fuck bro, I hope they pick me one year to do that NFX-3300 race. I'd win with my 'Little Miss Scarlett' here," the quarterback fantasizes.

Suddenly, police lights appear behind them. Blake didn't see the speed trap he passed a half-mile back. He thinks about not stopping but decides wisely and pulls over to the side of the turnpike—the police car parks behind him. After a few seconds, the police officer exits his vehicle and cautiously approaches the Maserati. Blake rolls down the window as the officer appears.

"Excuse me, gentlemen. Do you know how fast you were going? There's no way you didn't feel some of that G-force in this rocket," he says, trying to add a little humor.

"I'm sorry, officer. I'm just trying to get to the stadium before 3:30 pm. It's an emergency," he explains.

"Holy fuck! You're Blake Powers and Trevor Kacey. I didn't recognize you at first. You guys shouldn't be driving this fast. You could get hurt or worse," the officer says.

"We know, officer, and I'm sorry. It's just that you wouldn't want Trevor playing for the Chicago Bears, would you?" he cleverly asks, realizing the cop is a huge Dolphins fan.

"I wouldn't wish that on my worst enemy. However, if you are traded to Chicago, then Taylor Quick won't be at our games anymore. She'll be Chicago's problem," the officer replies.

"Well, Chicago already has plenty of problems. Number one is that they're in Chicago. Anyway, if we don't make it to the stadium by 3:30 pm, then Trevor is a Bear. He's breaking up with that cheating bitch today," Blake tries to explain.

"Oh yeah, that shit's all over the internet. Sorry, Mr. Kacey, but the Dolphins are back, baby! There's nothing worse than having to play for Chicago, except maybe the Vikings," the officer says while mimicking like he's puking.

"Absolutely, but officer, we do need to go. I'm sorry to rush you," he pleads.

"No problem, Mr. Powers, you guys follow me. A police escort to the headquarters front door courtesy of the Miami Police Department," the officer replies.

"Fuck yeah! Miami's finest right there. Tickets to the game are on me, sir," Blake shouts to the officer as he returns to his police cruiser.

"Dolphins, baby! TayTrev is done! The jinx is over!" The officer yells with excitement.

Week 15 has arrived, and the Miami Dolphins, coming off their bye week, are battling the Chicago Bears at Hard Rock Stadium. The score is close, with less than a minute left to play. The ball is snapped, and the quarterback drops back to pass. The football is released and soars 29 yards into the end zone to a wide-open Trevor Kacey.

Touchdown!

The Miami Dolphins take the lead 28-24 with only 38 seconds on the clock. It was a perfect strike from Blake to Trevor. The Dolphins are on the way to winning their 8th straight game and are in a wild-card spot with an 8-6 record with three games to play. Taylor Quick can't be seen at Miami Dolphin games anymore, and her face no longer dominates the NFL coverage airways. Fans are filling the seats at Hard Rock Stadium, and television viewership has increased. Trevor Kacey's stats have been fantasy football-worthy over the past eight games, scoring nine touchdowns in that span.

All is right in the sports world again!

Meanwhile, Taylor Quick and the new beau, Cunway East, have announced a new joint US tour for the upcoming year titled "The CunTay Tour." Miami is not scheduled as one of the cities where they'll be performing.

SIN CITY MADNESS

A couple of years ago, I shared my "Sin City Secret" that my friends and I researched during Valentine's Day in Las Vegas. For all you single guys who read my article in *Ear Pleasure* magazine, I hope you've had success with the hotties during your trip. This year's annual Valentine's Day guy's trip to Vegas didn't happen. The "Shiver Club," the name we gave ourselves, derives from what a group of sharks is called, was on hiatus for many reasons.

Samir Nazari and Taylor Quick were fresh off their divorce. Unfortunately, their highly publicized fizzled marriage became headline news and threw him further into the spotlight. All of the "Quickies" wasted no time blaming Samir for the failed marriage, even though she cheated on him with Hollywood actor Preston Harding. She's now dating NFL player Trevor Kacey. Naturally, Samir wasn't up for some Valentine's Day fun. Even though it was precisely what he needed.

Danny Whitehall joined a nature retreat group, "The Branch Elonians," who are into rock climbing, camping, and group sex. It took Danny about 8 months to finally realize he was a sex slave for a cult. He recently broke free from their retreat outside of Gainesville, Florida. He has a few interview scenes in the upcoming documentary "CULTure: Sex and Control" on *NetFux*. The limited series is about how cults are powered by sex to control their followers. He's now paranoid that the older couple he met at a Tesla dealership and are the creators of "The Branch Elonians" is going to kill him for escaping and becoming a whistleblower.

Scott Summers got fired from his job, not for having sex with his boss, he was recommending "inappropriate movies" to his work colleagues. They were uncomfortable around him because of his taste in films. Scott never passes up a good action film with explosions and raunchy sex. He couldn't attend the Valentine's Vegas trip last month because his new job at *Victor's Hush-Hush* did not give him the time off during their busiest month of the year. The world's leading and only men's lingerie retail chain drives more sales in January and the beginning of February than the other months combined. Scott's the store manager and is required to work six days a week from January 2nd to February 15th.

The last time I heard from Juan Cardoza was about 4 months ago. He was going through a rough patch with his 9th wife. Don't ask me her name; I can't keep up. They may be divorced now, and he might even be on wife number ten. I texted him a few days ago, reminding him of our annual March Madness guy's trip called "Sin City Madness." He didn't respond, so I wondered if that was still his number. We're sure he's still alive because he started a TikTok series of trying out and rating all the taco restaurants in Las Vegas. He has 11 followers, probably all of his ex-wives.

I broke up with my girlfriend about three months ago and went to Vegas alone during Valentine's Day this year since the gang could not reconnect. My article must have been popular because there were more single guys this year than any other. Besides, it wasn't the same without the "Shiver Club" with me; I also learned that turtlenecks are still out of style and shouldn't be worn during Vegas nightlife. I came across as a lonely and creepy guy, and women would put their hands over their drinks when I walked by.

Although Valentine's Vegas this year was a bust, I got "The Shiver Club" together a month later for our other annual guy's trip to Vegas… March Madness. This trip isn't focused on meeting hotties and getting laid. The reason is the NCAA men's basketball March Madness opening 4-day weekend, one of the most exciting and crazy sports events in the world. We still play our "Hottie Draft" and wouldn't say no to some pussy, but it's more challenging because it's mostly a "Dudefest" in Vegas that weekend.

At 3:17 a.m. on Thursday morning, 17 minutes behind schedule, we pack up in Samir's brand-new midnight black Infiniti QX80 luxury SUV to begin our journey to Sin City. We want to arrive in Vegas before the tip-off of the first game at 9:20 a.m. Samir has used his wealth and unwanted fame to book us a table for 6 at the newly renovated sports book in *The*

LinQ Hotel and Casino from 9:00 a.m. to 3:00 p.m. of the opening two days, Thursday and Friday, of March Madness. We get to enjoy all you can eat and drink for only $200 a person. We're excited to try this new location instead of at *Blondies* sports bar in *Planet Hollywood* hotel, like our previous years. They've always treated us well with excellent service and knock-out waitresses, but we wanted a change of pace this year.

This year, we have a new "Shiver Club" member accompanying us to Money Country. He's Samir's brother-in-law and accountant, Raimondo Zahir, better known as the "Razor" for short, within our group. Razor is happily married to Samir's wonderful sister, Lida Zahir, so he doesn't accompany us on our Valentine's Day trips. Razor is known for his constant desire to take selfies and disappear to a "Let it Ride" poker table in a casino.

Samir gets behind the wheel and begins to reverse out of Razor's driveway. I'm sitting in the passenger seat to his right while Scott and Danny are in the first row of backseats. Lida is outside the front door waving goodbye, as she always does. I roll down my window and inform her that Razor is already fast asleep in the second row of back seats.

"Well, that didn't take long," she giggles.

The drive is long but goes by fast as we joke, plan out the trip, and talk March Madness. Danny shares stories of his days of being a cult "Sex Slave" and how he's about to be famous after the *NetFux* documentary is released. We all agree, but we're not sure it will be the fame he wants. Samir doesn't want to discuss his famous marriage with Taylor, so we don't want to press him about it. Scott talks about how he was fucking his old boss, enjoys selling men's lingerie, and how comfortable men's thongs actually are.

"TMI, Scott, TMI!" Samir says.

As I'm telling the guys how much Vegas sucked without them this year during Valentine's Day, we catch Razor taking selfies of himself with the mountains by Hoover Dam as a background.

"How many selfies is that already Razor, 100?" Scott asks.

"No, just my first one. Guys, I don't take that many selfies." He replies, as we all laugh.

"Nah, not that many at all. Only about every 100 feet we walk on the strip." Danny explains while still laughing.

"Yeah, it takes us an hour to go from Harrah's to the Flamingo, making sure you're still with us after stopping for a selfie every 10 seconds, Razor. That's normally only a 2-minute walk." Samir quips.

The guys make it a mission to try and sneak into Razor's pictures to photo-bomb him without his knowledge. Razor only notices it days or weeks later when reviewing his photographs. Last year I got a text from Razor in July, four months after our trip, of his selfie at the Bellagio's gardens with me photo-bombing him with a caption: "Dammit, I didn't even see you there. LOL".

We arrive at *The Cromwell's* parking lot at 8:12 a.m. and unload our bags to check in early. Samir got us a 3-bedroom suite for the trip with a full bar, pool table, and hot tub—a perfect room for this weekend's madness. Oh, did I mention that Friday is also St. Patrick's Day? We will live up to one of our favorite Sin City mottos this weekend: "Vegas. Get your stupid out!"

We arrive at the room and claim our sleeping arrangements. Of course, Samir gets the master bedroom as he should. Scott and Danny share the room with 2 queen beds, and Razor is quite happy with the couch bed but stores his clothes in the master bedroom with Samir. I get the room with a single queen-sized bed, but I have the best view from my window... The fucking parking garage behind the *Cromwell*. Oh well, it's not like I'll be taking in the sights that much from here anyway.

I finally got a text from Juan in response to the one I sent him earlier this morning, telling him when and where we would be this morning.

Hey bros... I'm downstairs in the lounge, ready to party.

I read it out loud to the guys while we were unpacking. There was a collective chuckle, knowing there was some kind of catch.

"So, one of three things has occurred: He's divorced again, his new wife is out of town, or he snuck out and can only hang with us for a couple of hours," Scott replies.

"Should we take bets?" Samir asks.

"I got $20 on he's divorced or separated again," I respond.

"No bet! That's a sucker's bet." Danny says.

I replied to the text, informing him we would be down in a few more minutes. He couldn't come up to the suite without one of us or the key.

After about 10 minutes of unpacking, freshening up, and taking a piss, we all start our journey downstairs to head over to the *LinQ*. We have to check in before 9:30 a.m. to the sports book, but we have plenty of time since it's not even 9:00 a.m. We meet up with Juan at the lounge, and he has 5 "Honey Hideaways," Honey Jack, and Coke waiting for us. Good man!

I would have won the $20 bet as Juan tells us that he's officially divorced as of 2 months ago. He also said that he's done with dating for now.

"Yeah, right! Until the next woman says hello to you. I'll be your best man again for, what would this be, the fifth time?" I say, not believing a word he says.

"So, you're gay now?" Scott asks.

"Fuck you guys. You know what I mean. I just need a break from the bitches. I can't afford to get married again." Juan states.

"Yeah, because I'm sure it's all their fault you keep getting divorced," Danny says.

We laugh and walk over to the *LinQ*, which is only a short distance away. However, we notice that Razor's already a few yards behind us, taking selfies in front of the "Wheel of Fortune" slot machine.

The gorgeous hostess named Jasmine, whom Samir is already flirting with, is taking us to our table on the patio overlooking the *LinQ Promenade*. This is a perfect location for the "hottie draft" and is in view of several TVs showing all the games. Several pieces of March Madness swag are on the table: T-shirts, hats, bead necklaces, little foam basketballs, and other small trinkets. A sign that says "Reserved for Samir Nazari" is placed at the center of the table.

"Here you gentlemen are. Have a great time. Maddie will be your server today." Jasmine says as she seats us.

"Thank you, Jasmine. Here's my card. Text me later. We have a bungalow tonight at *Drai's Nightclub*," Samir says as he hands her his business card.

She takes the card with a blushing smile and walks away. We all stare at Samir, except Razor, who is busy taking a selfie of his location.

"What?" Samir asks as he sees us just staring at him.

"When the fuck did you get business cards made up?" I ask him.

"I got them last week. They just have a QR code that automatically locks my name and number in their phone's contacts," Samir explains.

"That's fucking genius. I need to get those cards for me." Scott says.

"Scott, your mom already has your phone number in her contacts." Danny jokes.

The first day of March Madness is crazy so far, not just in the NCAA games being played but also in Vegas. There have been quite a few upsets, with fans loudly cheering for their teams or hoping their bets will win. The college basketball point spread can be friend or foe.

Maddie, our server, is fantastic and very cute. She makes sure we have full drinks and food to eat. We placed the plastic bucket our swag was in across the room during the games and threw our mini-foam basketballs at it. A few other tables of patrons joined in, too, and soon, the room was raining tiny brown foam basketballs. Maddie and another server have fun retrieving the balls and throwing them back to us. Now that is service.

We're having a blast watching the games at the *LinQ* sports book and playing the "Hottie Draft," which Razor is especially bad at. We try to explain how to pick out the hot women walking by when it's his turn, but he manages to find only the less attractive. His poor play has cost him to lose the first 4 games and pay for a round of drinks each time. Samir won the first 2 rounds, Scott the 3rd, and I won that last round. Danny's placed 2nd three times, and Juan is content with picking "Fun 5s" and scoring in the middle of the pack each round.

We start the fifth and final game before heading out and finding another place to watch the games. Razor is up first; he gets really excited when a gorgeous woman walks by with a couple of other cute friends.

"That one. She's my pick. She's a perfect 10!" he shouts, pointing right at her without tact.

"Razor, calm down. You don't want her to hear you. Plus, she's like an 8 or 8 ½.," Juan says, while the rest of us score her a 7.

However, it's too late. She saw him pointing in her direction. Razor lines up his phone for a selfie with her in the background and notices on his cell phone screen that she is quickly approaching.

"What the fuck did you say about me, creep?" the woman loudly asks.

Razor was shaking with embarrassment and fear. Samir jumped in and used his charm to explain what was going on and that she was the best score he got all day—a 7, but he said 9. She's flattered and gives Samir her number to meet up later at *Drai's Nightclub* with her two friends, a fun 5 and a 6, if you're wondering.

For those who don't know what the "Hottie Draft" is because you didn't read my short story "Sin City Secret," then shame on you, but here's a short version. We play the "Hottie Draft" game, taking turns drafting women walking by. Each man gets 2 minutes to draft a woman of his choice, and the other guys score her from 1 to 10 for 5 rounds; the highest score wins. For more rules, pick up a copy of "Tales from the H1d3away" on Amazon and read my story there... Shameless plug.

Our next stop before returning to the room to prepare for dinner and *Drai's Nightclub* is the *Candy Martini Bar*, located upstairs in the *I Love Sugar* store attached to the *Flamingo* Hotel. This place is a hidden gem with some fun drinks. The hostess sits us at a table next to five women who are having a blast. They're all wearing University of Texas gear and celebrating their teams' win earlier today with two large $45 shareable candy martinis. Samir doesn't waste time.

"Nice win today, ladies. Congrats!" he says to the ladies.

"Thank you, sir. We are very happy with today's outcome," one of the women responds.

"National champs' baby!" another one yells out.

We all chuckle and think it's cute that they think Texas will win the NCAA basketball championship. Also, we're surprised and excited that there is actually a "girl's trip" to March Madness. During this weekend, Vegas is primarily a Dudefest!

We get our giant martinis and continue to flirt with the ladies next to us. The leader of the group is Tammy, a cute redhead. Scott is practically drooling over her. I find Whitney, a light-skinned black woman, extraordinarily sexy and equally returning of flirts. Juan is hitting up the cute Asian Indian woman, Varsha. The other blonde white girls, Holly and Erin, are chatting with each other.

I notice Danny sitting at the table, smiling and winking at an older couple in their 50s seated at the bar. I nudge Samir to get his attention to see what is happening. A minute later, Danny gets up and joins the older couple at the bar. Razor is taking selfies with the giant drinks, and I sneak in a photo bomb he doesn't catch again.

After returning from the day's activities, getting ready for the evening, and having a nice dinner at *CUT by Wolfgang Puck* Steakhouse in the Venetian, we head back to the Cromwell to check into *Drai's Nightclub*. The short walk from the Venetian to the Cromwell at night on the strip is always entertaining. We watch the pictures-for-money-seeking showgirls shouting at drunk guys who are not paying them for the photographs.

One poor guy passes us in tears, saying to himself, "Fucking Kentucky. Why did I bet so much on them? My wife is going to be pissed." Scott stops him and just gives him a big hug. The guy accepted it and didn't want to let go.

"Scott, either take him back to the room or get your ass over here," Danny yells as we keep walking.

Scott breaks free from the soon-to-be-divorced man and catches up to us. He doesn't notice that he passes Razor taking a selfie with the Las Vegas High Roller Observation Wheel in the background, and with perfect accidental timing, he ends up in the picture blocking the wheel. Razor didn't notice.

We finally arrived at the entrance of *Drai's Nightclub*, and we didn't have to wait in line because of the VIP status Samir had hooked us up with. Razor isn't into the club scene and decides to leave the group.

"Have fun, guys, I'm going to play some Let it Ride." He says as he starts walking away towards the casino game tables.

"Razor, don't play any of the sucker side bets like you always do!" Samir reminds him.

We are escorted to the bungalow and meet our knock-out of a waitress. She's about 5'6" with a killer body and a smile that melts all of us.

"My name's Christina, and I'll be taking care of you gentlemen this evening. Anything you'd like to start with to drink?" she asks.

"Great to meet you, Christina. You can call this the *Fungalow* for the rest of the night." I say, throwing the first witty, or at least I think it is, flirtation jab before Samir gets to it.

She gives me a pity chuckle. Juan is just shaking his head in disbelief that I said such a terrible line. Again, I thought it was pretty good. We order our drinks, and Christina walks away.

"*Fungalow*? Really dude? Did you forget how to pick up women? Even Scott has better lines than that." Danny says.

"Yeah, man, that was severely disappointing. I'm surprised they didn't kick us out after that comment. She's like, never heard that one before," Scott adds.

"Great, now we're labeled as the *Fungalow* guys from Ohio or some lame Midwest state. I'll have to tip her more to compensate for that garbage." Samir piles on as they all keep laughing and teasing me.

"Yeah, yeah. She laughed. So, it was a good line." I say, trying to defend myself, already replaying it in my head and realizing I deserve the punishment.

After a couple of drinks, more people are filling up the nightclub, and celebrity DJ Kid Kastaway is spinning great tunes that have the dance floor bumping. Scott, Juan, and Danny dance in the sea of glitter, pleather, and muscles. Samir spots the *LinQ* sports book hostess, Jasmine, and her friend. He calls her to the *Fungalow*... yeah, I'm sticking with it; get off my back! She introduces us to her friend, Courtney. She's a short, cute blonde that you can find about sixty of in this place, but no complaints. Jasmine is the big catch with her bronze skin, dark hair, and perfect body. Of course, Samir is already going in for the kill, sitting next to her on the couch and pouring her a drink. I strike up a conversation with Courtney, but she's more interested in the wave of heads going up and down on the dance floor. So, I invite her to dance.

It is approaching 2 a.m., and the place is still hopping with new and old faces from when we arrived. The girls from Candy Martini Bar have joined us, along with a couple of guys, Mark and Kevin, whom we invited to join us in the *Fungalow*. They told us the fantastic story of how they became best friends by surviving being chased by some Alabama rednecks, kidnapped by a crazy old couple, nearly killed a few times, and eventually rescued by the FBI during the national title game last year in Alabama.

The group of us is taking shots, talking, and coming and going from the dance floor, except for Danny, who's on the back couch and engaged in a tongue threesome with Kurt and Beth. You remember them, the older swingers couple from the *Candy Martini Bar*. They're actually super friendly, and I can't help feeling happy for Danny on this one.

Everyone is back in the *Fungalow* and it's a bit crowded but has its own party going on within the nightclub. Samir pours everyone a shot to finish off the bottle of "whatever the fuck we're drinking."

"To a great night, new friends, and the craziness that will happen back in our suite. Let's go, everyone!" Samir toasts and leads the way back to the suite.

We all pile into the elevator to the suite. Samir, not Razor, takes a great selfie of the large group of drunk and horny people. I press the floor button to our suite, but Danny presses the 5th floor button.

"What are you doing? We're going to the suite." I ask.

"I'm Sorry, bro. Kurt and Beth are taking me back to their room. See you in the morning," Danny informs me.

I don't say anything and am a little bit jealous he's going to have a nice quiet, and hot threesome with the sexy older couple while I have no fucking clue what's about to happen to me. The elevator opens, and the private threesome sneaks off, and we continue to the top floor.

I wake up to the sounds of somebody heaving in the bathroom. The blinds were left open, so the morning sun had found its way into my room. The sun's rays reveal a bunch of naked people on the bed and floor. Laying next to me is Whitney and Holly. I give myself a pat on the back for that successful score. I notice Scott sitting on the chair, and he's getting a blow job from Tammy, leader of the *Candy Girls*. That's what we named them at the club last night. He looks over and gives a huge cheesy grin and a thumbs up like he's a fighter pilot at the end of 'Top Gun.'

I get up and investigate who's most likely making a mess in the bathroom. I see Mark holding Erin's hair back while vomiting into the toilet, surprisingly not making a mess.

"Sorry, bro, I'll clean it up," Mark says

I walk out to see the damage in the living room area. I see poor Razor sleeping on the sofa bed, still in last night's attire, with his phone in his hand and a selfie of him sleeping. Which means when he got back in last night, and everyone was either fucking or passed out.

I slowly peek into Danny and Scott's room and see that Kevin's passed out on a bed, and nobody else is there. Samir comes out of his room to get water from the refrigerator. He grabs three bottles of water and walks back, not even noticing me standing there.

"Bro, who's in there with you?" I finally speak out.

"Oh fuck, you scared me. I didn't even see you there. I got Jasmine and Courtney in here, and we're about to shower. Great night, brutha!" he replies.

"OK, cool. Have fun. I don't see Juan and Varsha anywhere." I stated that I realized they were not anywhere in the suite.

"They probably got married," Samir jokes as he returns to the bedroom where the two honeys are waiting.

We agreed yesterday that we would meet at the *LinQ* sports book reserved table no matter what happened last night. Since it's St. On Patrick's Day, everyone is required to wear green. The only one missing is Juan, so I texted him to see if he was OK. He replies, "On my way. Be there in 10."

The first game tips off, and the excited, hungover crowd cheers. Jasmine, who managed to get home, shower, and show up to work on time, seats us. We have Maddy as our waitress again and give her some shit for not showing up to the club last night. She gives us some lame excuse that we make even more fun of.

"Shut up, guys. It's true. I had to babysit my younger sister while my parents went out last night. But what's going on tonight?" she asks.

"We'll be at TAO nightclub tonight. I got us a table for 10, and you're coming. Bring that cute waitress who was with you yesterday." Samir says, handing her his business card.

"That was Britney. She just broke up with her boyfriend, so she'll need a night out. We'll be there." Maddie says, walking away with our Bloody Mary and breakfast orders.

"Hey Samir, are you inviting Jasmine and Courtney tonight? I'd like to invite Kurt and Beth if you guys don't mind. They live here in Vegas." Danny asks.

"Yeah, I'll invite them. That Courtney chick was wild and did some crazy shit to me and Jasmine. I'm good with you inviting them. They were cool but might miss the Murder She Wrote convention at the Tropicana tonight." Samir jokes.

"Yeah, I heard they'll have the surviving cast members from Matlock Golden Girls. Oh wait, there aren't any because they're all dead." Scott adds.

"Ha ha, funny, but last night was special. We made love, laughed, wept, and cuddled all night." Danny defends.

We just stare at him for a few seconds and start laughing. Even Razor gets into the fun.

"Dude, that's gay," Razor says, making us laugh more, coming from the only married guy in the group.

We see Juan approaching the sports book and our table a few minutes later. He's holding hands with Varsha. I stand corrected; Razor is only one of two married guys in the group. They're flashing their left hand at us to show off their new wedding rings.

"Juan, do you buy a new ring for every wife, or is that the same one every time?" Scott asks jokingly.

"That's right, we got married early this morning. She's finally the one, guys." Juan brags and kisses her.

"Sure thing, Juan! We can tell by your bright, glowing smile. A couple of things, though: Why weren't we invited to the wedding? Also, this is a guy's trip. There are no women for game time, only during the night. She has to go." Danny reminds Juan of the rules.

"She knows. We just wanted to show you guys. We already showed the rest of the Candy Girls this morning when they returned to their hotel room. She's got plans with them at the spa. I'll see you later, my sexy curry dish," Juan says as he kisses her goodbye.

"I'll see you tonight, my delicious chorizo taco," she returns, walking away.

"Seriously, dude, you both pet-named each other off your ethnic foods. I don't know if that's racist or just gross." Scott says.

"Ahh, are you jealous? My cute little Shepard's pie!" Juan teases back, trying to tickle Scott.

"Damn, does that mean all the Candy Girls are coming too, then? That Tammy chick uses too many teeth while giving head. Felt like she was raking leaves. My dick has scrap marks on it," Scott says.

"That's herpes!" Razor responds.

"So that means your dick is like a brittle dried-up dead leaf on the ground!" Danny adds.

"I don't mind if they come. Whitney is gorgeous and fun, I wouldn't complain about another night with those girls," I reply.

"Oh no, He's in love already. Did you already to promise to visit her in Texas or pay for her to come see you in Phoenix?" Samir jokes.

"Ahhh, no! Don't be crazy." I respond.

All of the "Shiver Club" laugh, realizing that I'm full of shit and did indeed talk to Whitney about visiting each other after Vegas. "Fuck you guys! At least I'm not marrying her," I say trying to deflect back to Juan getting married again as my only defense.

Another great day of winning our bets, eating great food, drinking, and meeting other people. We're about to top it off at *TAO's* nightclub in the Venetian. We usually like to meet new women, but the women we hung out with last night were fun and hot. Plus, like I said, Vegas during March Madness can be a "Dudefest.", so you better take what you can get. However, the club is jumping with a lot of beautiful Bettys. Samir gets lucky and books the table next to billionaire Sid Sanderson. We know him from all of his hit porn movies, and he is the owner of *NetFux and Majestic streaming services.* Samir doesn't waste time and introduces all of us to him. He is with a couple of women that look familiar. They are "Minxy" Anders and "Candee Cane" Sunberg, his former porn co-stars. Sid quickly requests the nightclub personnel to combine both tables into one fun section.

I spot Hollywood actor Preston Harding and give him a wave, hoping he remembers us from last year's Valentine's crazy night. He doesn't and just ignores my gesture.

"This is the sexiest woman on the planet that will one day marry me, Tara 'Minxy' Anders. This beautiful thing here is the sensational Ashley 'Candee Cane' Sundberg. Finally, this is..." Sid introduces but is cut off by Scott.

"Lil' Tea Money! I know all your work. To me, you are one of the biggest, I mean, best midget porn stars ever. Your performance with Mr. Sanderson in his eleventh film, 'Big Trousers in Little Jhina,' was worthy of an award." Scott shouts, clearly star-struck.

"Thank you, sir. I no longer perform in the adult industry and am currently the head of Mr. Sanderson's security. So, even though Sid joined the tables, against my wishes, I require you all to stand at least 3 feet away from Mr. Sanderson.

Lastly, since you're a true fan of mine, I'll give you a free pass, but if you call me a midget again, I will break your neck," Lil' Tea Money instructs.

"You can reach that high?" Danny asks, and Lil' Tea Money furiously charges at him, but Sid holds her back.

"Oh, relax, Lil' Tea. I trust these guys. That's Danny Whitehall, star of the upcoming documentary, 'CULTure: Sex and Control' on *NetFux*. Plus, that's Samir Nazari, now ex-husband of Taylor Quick," Sid says, surprising us that he recognized Samir and Danny.

"You know who I am?" Danny shouts in shock.

"Of course, Danny, I thought the brutal honesty of your time in that cult was remarkable. Not everyone can admit on camera about the different things shoved in their ass countless times and start to enjoy it like you did." Sid replies.

The drinks keep flowing, the stage lights keep shining, the bodies keep bouncing, and the music is flowing. The group is all over the place in the nightclub. I'm dancing with Whitney, and she's making out with another girl she just met. The two THC gummies and a small line of coke I snorted are in full effect. This is going to be another epic night...

My eyes slowly open, and everything is blurry for the first few seconds. I'm not in my bedroom or even our suite. I climb over the naked sleeping Whitney, "Candee Cane" Sunberg, the chick from the dance floor, and who I think is one of the bouncers from *TAO*. I walk over to the giant window and pull the curtain open to expose the Vegas strip in its morning glory. I can tell by the location of the view that we are in a suite at the Cosmopolitan, a trip I don't recall making last night. Two women from Razor's selfie incident the other day are on the sofa lounger by the window, and the light wakes Razor's "Perfect 10" up. Looking at her now in this light, I downgrade my seven to a "Fun 5".

"Hey, stud, close that, please." She says and falls back asleep.

The living room has numerous other bodies lying around sleeping. On the couch, I see Danny and Beth going down on Kurt. He seems happy. Scott is passed out on the floor with Tammy asleep with his dickhead still in her mouth. I can't unsee the scrap marks on his dick now. I throw up a little in my mouth.

I walk into another room, thinking it is the bathroom. Samir is engaging in doggy-style sex with Jasmine with a couple of the Candy Girls, Erin and Holly, playing next to them.

I hear Varsha letting Juan have it out in the hallway, so I decide to leave that alone. Now, I must know what else occurred in this massive suite. There are a few faces I don't recognize sleeping throughout the place that we must have picked up at the club. I open the door to the master bedroom. Sid is on his phone, sitting up in his bed. "Minxy" Anders, Maddy, Britney, and Courtney are lying next to him.

"Hey buddy, come on in. Have a seat on the bed." Sid invites.

I don't hesitate and accept. I walk over and carefully sit on the bed, trying not to wake one of the sleeping beauties. I accidentally kick a small lump at the end of the bed, and suddenly, Lil' Tea Money pops out of the sheets and starts yelling at me.

"Watch where you put those stanky ass feet mutha fuckah! Why are you in here anyway? This is Mr. Anderson's private chambers." Lil' Tea Money shouts!

"That's enough, Lil' Tea. Why don't you check on all our guests out there and ensure everyone is safe and comfortable." He orders.

Lil' Tea Money carefully jumps off the high bed and walks out of the room, still naked but in command.

"I have to say I really loved your 'Sin City Secret' story in your book, which I just bought this morning," Sid acknowledges.

"You bought and read my book this morning? I don't even remember telling you I was an author." I reply.

"Yeah, you bragged about Valentine's Day being the best time to get laid in Vegas in the club last night. You said you published a story about it. So, I woke up this morning and ordered it on Kindle. I haven't read all of it yet, just the first 3 stories," Sid answers.

"Thank you so much. I hope you enjoy the rest of it," I reply with embarrassment and excitement as I think *a billionaire bought and is reading my book.*

Courtney wakes up and just starts making out with me. Sid smiles and goes back to reading my book. The foreplay starts waking up the other women in bed, and we begin a fantastic Saturday morning orgy, except only the ladies are allowed to touch Tara "Minxy" Anders. A rule that I'm more than willing to be obliged to follow. Especially with two women, and now Lil' Tea Money, all over me. And now I'm thinking to myself, *I'm having an orgy with women and the billionaire that is reading my book.* I believe I am one step closer to becoming a World-Famous Author.

"I'm thinking this will make your next book?" Sid says with "Minxy," riding him in reverse cowgirl style.

6 months later.

I'm still dating Whitney, long distance, of course, so we'll see how that goes. Mr. Sid Sanderson bought the rights to my book and plans to make an anthology series to air on *NetFux* or *Majestic*. Now, I can pay for the rooms in Vegas.

Scott was promoted to district manager of *Victor's Hush-Hush*, and we're pretty sure he's having sex with his regional manager, Tawny Niro.

Danny's enjoying his 15 minutes of fame from "CULTure: Sex and Control" and living a happy polyamorous life with Kurt and Beth in Las Vegas.

Samir is following his passion and has opened a delicious Michelin-star Mediterranean restaurant in Downtown Phoenix called "The Shiver Club." Brought a tear to our eyes when he told us the name.

Razor submitted his selfies to the Guinness Book of World Records and now holds the title "Most Selfies with Photo Bombs." Lida is so proud of him.

Juan and Varsha filed for a marriage annulment the next day because he wanted to include Erin in a threesome that night in Sid's suite. There goes wife # 10, this one in record time.

BOX BOX, PUSH PUSH

The 22 drivers in Formula 2, or F2 for short, are vying to become the next driver promoted to Formula 1, also known as F1. Formula racing is one of the fastest-growing sports in the world. So, winning an F2 championship can be just the ticket for one of those rare and coveted F1 cockpits. Marc "The Flying Dutchman" Van Straten is one of those lucky chosen few. He's already wrapped up the F2 championship with three races ago. He will leave for the Formula 1 circuit to drive for the *Red Bullet* team after this final race at Yas Island in the United Arab Emirates. Although he doesn't need to win this race to prove anything, he wants to show pure dominance and put the rest of the F1 drivers on notice for next season. Marc also wants to perform well for his current team, *Blackburn Motorsports*, and their crew, many of whom are his friends.

The weather for today's race could be better, with the slight drizzle making the track slick in certain turns. The cars will have full wet tires to help control those slippery areas of the track and avoid crashing or spinning out. The stands are still full of excited fans holding umbrellas, wearing rain jackets, and, of course, the shirtless fanatics with their favorite driver's car number painted on the chest. However, the painted numbers are no longer legible after a few minutes in the rain. The fans don't seem to care.

Marc, known for his aggressive driving, is sitting in pole position with his number one rival, Francisco Calderon of the *Wilcox F2 team*, who is only two cars back after yesterday's qualifying results. These two drivers have battled all season, but in the end, the *Blackburn* car and Marc's experience was too much for Francisco to overcome. This is only Francisco's 3rd year in F2, and he has already secured runner-up for the season but still wants to beat Marc before he leaves for F1. Bragging rights go a long way in this sport.

Francisco's teammate, best friend, and secret lover is Logan Wilcox, currently nestled between the two rivals with the

2nd spot in pole position. He's the son of the billionaire and team owner of the *Wilcox F1* and *Wilcox F2* racing teams, Theodore "Teddy" Wilcox. Francisco and Logan have talked about coming out and telling the world of their relationship, but Logan is hesitant. He fears his father's disapproval and how the racing world would react. Francisco is close to making an F1 team, and Logan doesn't want to be the reason he's held back. This is Logan's 1st year on F2, but the experts see much potential. His love for Formula 1 led to him racing as a young boy and teenager in the karting circuits, finally working his way into a Formula-style car at 20. Teddy Wilcox wanted to support his son's passion and dream, so he bought a Formula 1 and 2 team... Toys for the rich, enjoyment for the fans.

The drivers sit anxiously for the red lights to disappear and start the race. The light drizzle of rain beating down on their helmets and cars will make for an exciting race. The special coating on their visors will allow them to see the track and fellow competitors, but it still poses some visual limitations.

The 1st red light turns on.

You could almost hear every driver's heart rate increase several beats a second. Marc is calm and mentally prepared to take care of business. Logan is nervous but has learned to control his nerves throughout the season. Francisco is plotting how to steer the vehicle to pass Logan and Marc in the first few seconds of the race, usually the craziest and most hazardous.

The 2nd red light turns on.

Marc is focused, staring at the empty track ahead of him. He knows winning the pole position gives him a considerable advantage. Logan stares at the back of Marc's car, hoping for one mistake by the champion that he and Francisco can take advantage of. Francisco rolls his shoulders back and forth to relieve some of the stiffness.

The 3rd red light turns on.

Almost every driver takes a deep breath and exhales simultaneously, as if synchronized. Marc's face smirks. Logan locks his eyes on the red lights, and Francisco grips the steering wheel tighter.

The 4th red light turns on.

The driver's nerves have taken a backseat to adrenaline and concentration. They all know it's just a matter of a few more seconds before they have to press down on that gas pedal and make their moves.

The 5th red light turns on.

The screaming fans, car engines, and the pitter-patter of raindrops fall silent to the young men's ears as they prepare to race for the last time this season.

The 5 red lights disappear.

The race begins, and smoke from burning rubber and engine exhaust fills the air. The 22 race cars jostle for position by swerving, bumping, breaking, and accelerating off the starting line. The most chaotic part of the race goes off without any significant incidents.

During the 38th minute, Francisco takes the lead from Marc with a swift move to the right of the season champion's car. However, the lead didn't last long as Marc's front right tire clipped Francisco's rear left tire. The touching of the synthetic tires, combined with the wet, slick track, caused Francisco's car to veer off the track and flip several times. The #29 car finally came to a stop, hitting the racetrack wall, and is now upside down. Francisco is trapped, with flames starting to appear from the engine. The safety team races to the car to assist in getting him out.

"Red Flag, Red Flag. Box, Box!" Logan hears his team principal say over the headset as he's currently in 4th place.

"Who crashed?" Logan asks frantically.

"Logan, just pass with caution and box. The safety crew is already on top of it," the team principal instructs.

Logan slowly passes the crash site, which was about 45 seconds ahead of him when the accident occurred. He lost time during his final pit stop and moved back into fourth. Logan sees the upside-down #29 *Wilcox* car engulfed in flames, with the safety crew desperately trying to extinguish the fire. He pulls off the track, stops, and climbs out of the vehicle.

"Logan! Logan! Get back into the car. Let the safety crew handle it before you get hurt," the Team principal commands.

He doesn't listen and runs over to the car. A few safety crewmen grab him and stop him from getting closer to the burning vehicle. Logan sees Francisco's helmet still upside down and in the cockpit surrounded by flames. He falls to the ground weeping heavily, knowing that his teammate, best friend, and love of his life is burning to death. He rips off his helmet and starts vomiting on the dirt.

After a long delay from the wreck cleanup, the race restarts and concludes 22 minutes later with the checkered flag waving as Marc "The Flying Dutchman" Van Straten zooms past the finish line, winning the final race of this F2 season. The victory is bittersweet for him, knowing he will move on to his new team next season, leaving his F2 friends, crew, and team behind. The victory also comes with some controversy and what will surely be a pending investigation. Logan didn't finish the race as he was disqualified for exiting his vehicle and placing himself in a dangerous situation. That didn't bother him, as he was already on the way to the hospital.

5 seasons later.

The fans are jumping with excitement for the start of the new F1 season here in Bahrain. The weather is perfect, and many celebrities are in attendance. Celebrity DJ Kid Kastaway took time off from his residency at *Drai's Nightclub* in Las Vegas to spin the tunes for the amped crowd before the start of the race. People are still filing in and finding seats before the five red lights vanish and the engines roar.

The popularity of F1 has grown so fast because of the *Netflix* series about the sport. The handsome drivers and drama behind the scenes help feed the spectators' interest. This season is up for grabs after the retirement of eight-time champion and racing legend Layton Hillman. Last year's runner-up, Marc "The Flying Dutchman" Van Straten, is the Las Vegas favorite to win this year's championship. He drives for the *Red Bullet* team, who won last year's Constructor's championship, despite Layton winning his eighth driver's championship, driving for team *Merced*.

Only in their 5th year in Formula 1 did the *Wilcox F1* team from the United States spark the interest of fans and experts this season, with billionaire Teddy Wilcox bringing his son Logan up from F2 to lead the team. The departure of team *Lotus* due to financial reasons 5 years ago opened the door for Teddy Wilcox to buy his way into the prestigious sport. He beat out billionaires Elon Musk, Larry Ellison, and Sid Sanderson, who were also trying to grab a piece of the popular F1 spotlight. Unfortunately, the *Wilcox F1* team has not been as successful as the *Wilcox F2* team in those 5 years. Logan has won multiple championships in F2 in the past few years, and he is determined to prove to his father that he's ready for F1 and dedicates every victory to Francisco. Once Logan arrived at the *Wilcox F1* team, he secured the #29 for his racing vehicle number. He had a small rainbow flag decal placed underneath the #29 with the initials "FC" in the middle to honor his deceased lover.

The race is about to begin in a couple of minutes, and the announcers are priming the television audience for a spectacular race.

"This will be an interesting start to the season, Layton. It's a little odd not seeing you out there this year," Says Derek LaRue, a 10-year broadcasting veteran and former F1 driver.

"Yeah, it's definitely a different feel up here in this spacious booth versus the small, tight confines of the cockpit. I don't miss that part of it," Layton responds.

"With your departure from the track, this year's championship seems wide open for the first time in many years. Who do you like to take home the championship?" Derek asks.

"Well, many experts have Van Straten winning, but I can't count out my teammate for the past 4 years, Russell Smith. Dark Horse could be the crafty older veteran for the *Delpine* team, Ricardo Gomez. I'm curious how this race will end up," Layton answers.

"The addition of Logan Wilcox this year, who surprisingly took 3rd place in qualifying, has brought a huge spike in the LGBTQ demographic to F1 fans. The tragic story of his former teammate and boyfriend, Francisco Calderon, convinced Logan to come out as a gay Formula One driver," Derek says.

"Absolutely, I applaud Logan for having the courage to announce his sexuality publicly and reveal his secret relationship with Francisco. The sport will only grow stronger because of this. He's sitting at 3rd and driving well. He's got a good chance at victory or at least a podium spot," Layton adds.

"Well, race fans, we're just a couple of minutes away from the start of the new Formula One season. The drivers and crews are making final adjustments. The fans are excited, the stars are partying in their expensive suites, and the networks prepare for race coverage. We'll be back after these messages for those 5 iconic red lights to go blank and wheels start spinning," Derek states.

"Ooh, look, there's Taylor Quick and her Miami Dolphins boyfriend Trevor Kacey. It's like we didn't see enough of them a few weeks ago at the Super Bowl," Layton says sarcastically as the television camera fixates on the celebrity couple before cutting away to commercial, but only after Layton's comment was caught on the air.

"Okay, Layton, we're off the air. Tell me what you really think? I don't think the 'Quickies' will like you after that comment," Derek says, partially joking and partially serious.

"Oh well, I'm only saying what most people think. Sports fans don't want to see her reaction to every exciting thing in sports. It was out of control during the Super Bowl. Do you know they showed her 47 times during the game and after?" Layton responds.

"Yeah, but she brings a new audience. A new audience increases attendance and viewership, bringing in more money. So on and so on," Derek explains.

"Not always a good thing, Derek. Just saying," the retired champion replies.

The engines are roaring as the drivers sit in their starting positions, waiting for the 5 red lights to appear individually, and then disappear to put the pedal to the metal. Marc Van Straten sits in pole position after completing the best time in qualifications yesterday. The following cars behind him are Logan Wilcox in 3rd and Van Straten's teammate, Saul Escobar, in the 2nd spot. The anticipation for the start of the race can be nerve-racking for most drivers. However, instinct, strategy, and a hint of caution kick in once that gas pedal is pushed down. Physically fit, mentally strong, balls of steel, a degree of narcissism, and a tiny bit of a death wish are requirements to be an F1 driver.

1st Red Light
Hands grip the steering wheels tighter.

2nd Red Light
A final look around at the cars close to them.

3rd Red Light
Quick sips of fluids from the driver's drinking system satisfy the dryness in their mouths caused by nerves and the sun's warmth.

4th Red Light
One last big sigh before pushing down on that gas pedal.

5th Red Light
The laser focuses on the 5 red lights before they disappear, and the cars accelerate from 0 to 60 in less than 3 seconds.

And they're off. The engine's roar, the crowd screams, and the new season of F1 has officially begun.

About 16 minutes into the race, Marc Van Straten has the lead by two seconds over Logan Wilcox, who overtook Saul Escobar at the start. Logan stares intensely at the back of Van Straten's car, focused on the *Red Bullet* decal. Logan replays the video of the "accident" in his head that he watched thousands of times over the past 5 years. After their investigation, that slight touch of wheels was deemed an "accident" by the F1 stewards. Logan believes otherwise. He knows that Van Straten felt threatened by Francisco's driving and wanted to teach him a lesson with a bit of tap, which turned into a tragic death. Logan doesn't think that Van Straten intended to harm or kill Francisco, just merely knock him out of that final race 5 years ago. He studied the exact spot those wheels touched to cause Francisco's car to go off course. Now, it was his turn to teach Van Straten a lesson.

"Wilcox and Van Straten are battling for first on the 11th lap and approaching the straight away. This could be where Wilcox makes his move," Layton comments.

"Push, Push!" Logan's team principal orders.

Logan speeds up and slides over to Van Straten's left side. His front tire is just inches from Van Straten's rear left tire.

"Push, Push! That's it, Logan!" his team principle encourages.

Logan slightly drifts just enough to touch Van Straten's tire just before turn 13. Logan eases back on the acceleration, and Van Straten's car is spinning out of control and veering off course. Logan remains on course and takes over 1st place. Van Straten's car slid sideways, and his tires hit a divot in the ground, causing his car, traveling over 200 MPH, to flip several times. The sight of debris and the sound of the vehicle hitting the ground is deafening to race fans nearby. Van Straten's car hits with full force against a guard wall, splitting the Formula 1 car in half.

The Red Flags are immediately waved, and the drivers are ordered back to their pits while the accident is cleared and the track is safe to drive on again.

"Box, Box, Logan!" *Wilcox F1* team principal instructs.

The safety team wasn't far from the crash site and immediately responded. An ambulance is ordered to take Van Straten's motionless body away. The race track is silent as everyone watches with fear and hope that Van Straten is not seriously injured.

Logan is already in his pit area and exits the car while his crew inspects it for damages and makes the required corrections. The drivers will use this time to hydrate, stretch, and review strategies with their teams.

"What happened there, mate? You, okay?" Logan's team principal asks.

"Yeah, I'm fine. I think our wheels touched. It looked like Marc was drifting into my area before the turn. I'm a bit shaken; I just need to take a short walk," Logan responded, turning away from everyone.

Logan walks past his Formula 1 car and feels the warmth coming off the vehicle's engine from the race. This causes him to look down and notice the rainbow flag decal with the beautiful letters "FC" in the middle, producing a diabolical grin.

THE GREEN SUITS

College mascots come in all shapes and sizes. Some are similar to cartoon characters like Arizona State University's *Sparky the Sun Devil* or the University of Oregon's *Duck,* based on *Donald Duck.* Then there are the odd ones, such as Ohio State University's *Brutus Buckeye* or Syracuse's *Otto the Orange.* Of course, some schools have the unexplainable mascot that leaves us scratching our heads. For example, try telling me what the fuck Western Kentucky University's *Big Red* is? Can you explain what Evergreen State College's *Speedy the Geoduck is?*

However, one university doesn't have an oversized mascot head or bulky furry suit that nearly causes the school-spirited student wearing one to pass out from heat exhaustion. The University of Notre Dame's *Leprechaun* is a specially selected student who wears no headgear to cover their face. They dress in a green tailcoat, a gold vest, and a green Irish country hat and carry a shillelagh stick (go ahead and google it; I'll wait...)

This is Jimmy O'Sullivan's first year at the prestigious catholic university, Notre Dame. He's been waiting his whole life to follow in the footsteps of his grandfather and father. His bright orange hair and extended goatee beard scream Irish catholic. At first glance, some people would guess that Jimmy is from Boston or somewhere around that heavily populated Irish catholic area. He hails from Phoenix, Arizona, where the summer sun is never kind to his fair pale skin. However, his grandfather, Patrick O'Sullivan, is originally from the Boston suburb of Dorchester, Massachusetts. Sometime in 1970, Patrick left the greater Boston area for his freshman year at Notre Dame. He would become the first in the O'Sullivan family to attend college. Until then, most O'Sullivan's became police officers, tradesmen, or fishermen. A few years later, during Patrick's senior year, he would win the coveted spot of Notre Dame's *Leprechaun* mascot during football season. Only a handful of loyal and dedicated students have been honored with this title since its inception in 1963. After graduation,

Patrick was offered a great position as senior sales manager for a large car dealership in Phoenix, Arizona. In the early 1980s, he would open O'Sullivan's Ford car dealership in Phoenix.

Nearly 30 years later, after Patrick led the cheers of the Notre Dame faithful, John David O'Sullivan, J.D. for short, would bring in the new millennium wearing the famous green suit on the sidelines of Notre Dame football. He was there during their epic Gator Bowl victory over UCLA on New Year's Day of 2000. His best friend and roommate, Oscar Hillman, was the star quarterback and eventually became godfather to Jimmy. He threw for 478 yards and five touchdowns in that game, which helped him get drafted by the Cleveland Browns in the fourth round of the NFL draft. Oscar would play four years in the NFL until retiring from an injury. He started acting and then moved on to directing.

During JD's junior year, he met Gwendolyn Harris, who was on the Notre Dame track team. They were married a year after graduation. The happy couple moved back to Phoenix, where JD would become heir to O'Sullivan's car dealership empire, which grew to five locations valley-wide. Gwen got a job coaching the ASU women's track team. Three years later, they gave birth to Jimmy.

J.D. wasted no time brainwashing Jimmy into Notre Dame football by having him sit in front of the T.V. watching games together throughout his childhood. Jimmy worshiped his dad and wanted to follow in his footsteps: go to Notre Dame, be the *Leprechaun* mascot, graduate, get married, and take over the family car dealership, which has now expanded to eight locations in Arizona.

When Jimmy first arrived to start his college career, the Notre Dame campus was overwhelming. Even though he had been to the campus as a kid with his father to attend a few football games and once for an official visit to get accepted, it was still a lot to take in. He stood looking up at the iconic mural "Word of Life," more commonly known as "Touchdown Jesus." His plans were underway, with phase one completed: get accepted into the University of Notre Dame.

Jimmy returns to his freshmen dorm, where he sees his roommate and family friend Spencer Hillman, a shy young black man dressed very fashionable, very L.A. He's putting up some movie posters on the wall by his bed.

"Hey Spence, how are you? I'm so glad we're roommates. I see you're putting up your dad's movies," Jimmy says.

"Well, I better put them up; he pays for my tuition and is a football hero around here," Spencer replies, finishing his wall décor.

"My favorite film by your dad is *East Haven,* based on the true story of the psychos in the insane asylum back in the 1970s," Jimmy says while pointing at the *East Haven* poster.

"Yeah, that's probably my favorite of his films, too. He's currently working on a movie based on those gay Florida State guys who got trapped on a tour bus with an alligator a couple of years back," Spencer reveals.

"That's awesome. Your dad is like the horror king of movies right now. I'm so glad to see you, buddy," Jimmy says.

The two roommates hug and continue to talk while Spencer finishes unpacking and decorating his side of the room.

The Notre Dame football home opener against Navy has sold out, and the fan energy is electric. The student section is among the loudest in recent years as the game is underway. Jimmy and Spencer are in the front row, dressed in green and gold. Notre Dame returns the opening kickoff for a touchdown, and the stadium filled with over 74,000 Fighting Irish fans is going wild. Spencer turns to high-five Jimmy, who is focused more on the Notre Dame sidelines than the game.

"Damn, Jimmy, you didn't even see that awesome touchdown. Do you have a crush on one of the cheerleaders or the *Leprechaun*? I don't blame you, I would let him show me his pot of gold or his lucky charm?" Spencer jokes with a poor attempt at an Irish accent.

"No, Spence, it's not a crush. You know that my goal and lifetime dream is to follow in my grandfather and father's footsteps and become the Notre Dame *Leprechaun*," he explains.

"I know, buddy. Let's make it happen. What's the first step to becoming the famous Notre Dame *Leprechaun?*" Spencer asks.

"They hold tryouts. The best three get picked, and the very best becomes the Gold team, which will be on the football and men's basketball sidelines. The Blue and Green cheer teams will attend smaller events, like badminton or women's hockey. The football games are the most prestigious and honored to perform at," Jimmy answers.

"When are the tryouts? I might add that they've already chosen this year's lucky *Leprechaun*—and a fine choice," Spencer says, gushing over the current mascot.

"End of the school year, they pick next year's winners through a competition by performing a skit, leading a mock pep rally, a push-up contest, and a media interview session," Jimmy answers.

"Well, we have about eight months to prepare and train you. Let's get started now. After the game, I can privately interview Mr. *Leprechaun* over there," he giggled.

"Shut up, you're so bad," Jimmy says as they laugh.

The two roommates and best friends continue to watch the game and the *Leprechaun's* every move. Jimmy will spend the rest of the school year attending events where the *Leprechaun*s appear. He will study and observe their movements and school spirit.

Jimmy meets Julie Atwood at a Halloween party a few months into his first year. She's a beautiful brunette from Florida majoring in pre-med. He's wearing a *Leprechaun* costume, of course. Spencer dresses as *Commando Clown*, one of the horror characters in his dad's film "East Haven," but he ditches Jimmy to play beer pong with a couple of cute guys. Julie's costume is a USC cheerleader zombie, which caught Jimmy's attention immediately. She is the prettiest woman and zombie in the room. Her roommate, Olivia Harris, is dressed as a sexy *Leprechaun*, if there is such a thing. She walks off to hang out with a couple of sorority girls, leaving Julie standing alone several feet away from Jimmy. They're both scanning the party for somebody to speak to. He decides to approach her and introduces himself. To his delight, she accepts his greeting. They immediately hit it off and spend the night talking about their plans, past, family, and anything else they could think of to keep each other company.

"Damn, I'm so glad I met you tonight, Julie. It's like I've known you forever. So weird, right?" Jimmy says, in awe of her beauty, even as a zombie.

"Yes, it's been a great night, and I look forward to seeing you tomorrow for lunch. I'm sorry, my roommate showed up as a *Leprechaun*, too. She has this life-long dream of being the Notre Dame *Leprechaun*, even if it's a male-dominated position," Julie says.

"Well, she will have tough competition because I'm going for that same position. My father and grandfather were Notre Dame *Leprechauns*, so it's a family tradition," he reveals.

"That's fucking awesome. I'll be cheering for you all the way then. As long as you don't fall in love with Olivia while you're both trying to become *Leprechauns*," she says jokingly.

"Don't worry, being a *Leprechaun* is a solo job. You don't see a bunch of *Leprechauns* flocking around together. They're a lonely bunch. So, why would you cheer for me over your roommate? And why shouldn't I fall in love with her?" Jimmy flirts heavily.

"Because she's a cunt!" She replies.

He spits out his beer, not expecting that response. That was the moment he fell in love with Julie Atwood and knew she was the one.

Jimmy's first year of college is coming to an end. There's only a month left, and this has been the best year of his life. He's met a lot of great people and made a ton of friends. Having Spencer as a roommate and meeting Julie has been the most significant part of his first year. They've helped him prepare for the *Leprechaun* tryouts this Friday. Jimmy feels like he's more prepared than anybody who seeks to be the coveted green-suited icon. *Stand-by world, Jimmy O'Sullivan is going to take college football sidelines by storm in the fall.*

Jimmy's sitting at his dorm room desk, finishing a paper due tomorrow. Spencer's lying in bed, playing Candy Crush on his phone. Jimmy takes out his cell phone, and he Facetimes his dad.

"Hey buddy, how's college life treating you? I can't believe you're almost finished with your first year," JD O'Sullivan says as he answers the call.

"It's Going great, Dad. I love it here. I'm going to miss everyone over the summer. Although I'll visit Spence in L.A., He's taking me to his dad's movie premiere. And Julie's going to fly out to Phoenix for a week," he responds excitedly.

"That's great, buddy. Tell Spence I say hello. Your granddad is here to watch the Suns playoff game," his dad says, pointing the camera at Patrick sitting on the couch.

"What's going on, little firehead? You banging a lot of that college ass like your grandpappy did?" Patrick O'Sullivan chimes in.

"Hey Grandpa, I have a girlfriend, so I'm not banging a lot of asses. You'll meet her this summer; she's super nice and smart," Jimmy says while rolling his eyes.

"You're a freshman; you should be screwing as many of those catholic girls as you can before getting a girlfriend. Dammit, J.D., these kids today get attached way too easily. I hope she's got great tits and ass, at least. What about Spencer? He hasn't tried to butt fuck you yet, has he?" Patrick asks.

"Grandpa, Spencer is my best friend, and gay guys don't go around randomly butt fucking other guys. Besides, you've known Spencer his whole life," he responds.

"Well, back in my day at Notre Dame, they didn't allow the gays and colored folks on campus. Just keep an eye on your stuff and your ass," Patrick says.

"Love you too, Papa O'Sullivan!" Spencer yells from his bed and laughs.

Jimmy looks at Spencer and says, "I'm sorry." Spencer, giggling, gives Jimmy a thumbs-up. He's used to Papa O'Sullivan's "Old Ways."

"Okay, Dad, that's enough sexism and racism today, sorry Spence. Never mind your Grandpa, he gets confused with his old age," J.D. responds as he points the camera back at him.

"I'm calling to let you guys know that my video submission for the tryouts that Spencer shot and edited was awesome, the letters of recommendation from you and Grandpa were perfect, and my resume all helped me become one of the finalists!" Jimmy reveals.

"Don't fuck it up, ginger; you have a tradition to uphold. Concentrate this week and go fuck a naïve freshman girl to loosen up!" Patrick yells from the background.

"Thanks, Grandpa, I'll see what I can do," he responds, shaking his head.

"Don't listen to him, and I'm glad we could help. I'm sure none of the other finalists have letters of recommendation from two former old-school *Leprechauns*," J.D. brags.

They say their goodbyes, and Jimmy ends the Facetime chat with his dad and "colorful" grandfather.

"Bro, your Grandpa is a hoot. He's always been cool with me. I know it's the dementia that causes him to say those things. I can't wait to see him again after one of his Klan meetings. What's up with the 'Ginger' and 'Fire Head' names? Those are new," Spencer says while laughing.

"He has moments where he forgets we're in the 2020s and not the 1970s. He always makes fun of my redhead, even though he and my dad have red hair, just not as bright as mine," Jimmy explains.

The eight finalists stand in the middle of the Notre Dame football field before the ten judges responsible for deciding who will become the three new *Leprechauns* for next year. The stadium is empty except for groundskeepers, cheerleaders prepping, and a few players warming up before Notre Dame's annual Blue-Gold spring game. Jimmy looks at Olivia, his biggest competitor, and she glances back. She mouths the words, "Fuck you". He ignores it and focuses his stare over the northern endzone to glimpse the top of the "Touchdown Jesus" mural. This is the moment it hits him: he's one of eight people left to be selected to become *the University of Notre Dame Leprechaun!*

"Okay, gentlemen and lady, you are the final eight selected for a shot to become the greatest college mascot of all time! We have considered your letters of recommendation, resumes, and videos. You survived yesterday's mock pep rally and media interview session last night. However, we'll see how you all do during an actual game today. You can all lead the student section during today's spring game. All eight of you will also do push-ups for every point scored by the Blue and Gold teams. I wish you luck, and we will see you back here at game time in a couple of hours," Latonya Jackson, head cheerleading coach, explains.

Jimmy notices a quick smile and wink from LaTonya to Olivia as everyone disperses and realizes the cheerleading coach favors her for the position. He knows this is a problem because LaTonya heavily influences the other judges. Jimmy doesn't just want to make the *Leprechaun* team; he wants that Gold team spot.

Jimmy meets Spencer and Julie at their favorite hangout, *O'Rourke's Public House* restaurant and pub. They sit in their lucky booth and order the usual. Spencer, Rueben Fritters with a Guinness. Julie, Power Salad with a pint of Angry Orchid. Jimmy, 4-Horsemen burger and no alcohol, just water today.

"Go get 'em' Jimmy!" one of the barkeeps yells from behind the bar in support of his quest.

"I think Olivia and Miss Jackson have a secret connection or agreement. I saw them smile and wink at each other in this morning's meeting. She's got the advantage," Jimmy says.

"Fuck, I was afraid of that. Her dad's a huge donor to the school and the booster club. I bet he paid off Miss Jackson and possibly others," Julie reveals.

"That's some B.S. Let me call my dad right now. He's a booster here, too, and can probably help. You should call your dad to Jimmy," Spencer says.

"Nah, don't worry about it. I'll outperform Olivia and win the spot. All the judges can't be paid off," Jimmy responds.

"You can't outperform money, bro. I'd be happy to call right now, say the word," Spencer says.

"Oh shit, I forgot I have a sorority meeting in 15 minutes. I'll see you guys at the game. You can have my salad and cider," Julie says as she quickly gets up, kisses Jimmy on the head, and leaves.

"I'm not eating that gross-ass healthy salad, are you? I'll drink the cider, though," Spencer says.

"No, I'll just get it to go and give to one of the homeless around campus on the way back to the stadium," Jimmy replies.

"Bro, hold the fuck up. Look who just walked in and sat at the bar: two other *Leprechaun* competitors. They just ordered drinks and a shot. Oh, hell yeah, watch this. Hey Carla, come here please," Spencer calls over the waitress.

Carla comes to their table to see what Spencer needs. She's their favorite waitress and always hooks them up with free drinks or discounts.

"What's up, Spence? I saw Julie run out. Is everything okay?" Carla asks.

"Yeah, it's all good. She has a meeting or something. Can you do me a huge favor, please? See those two guys at the bar? Can you buy them two shots each from me?" Spencer reveals his plan.

"Ahh, you sneaky devil. I know what you're doing. Get them drunk so they can fail the *Leprechaun* test later today. Well, I like it! 2 shots coming right up for the finalists," Carla responds positively to the plan.

"Spencer, I want to win this fair and square," Jimmy says.

"Hey, they came in and ordered drinks. They don't have to do the shots if they don't want to," Spencer defends his decision.

The two men cheer each other and down the shots they bought. The barkeep delivers two more shots and their beers. He tells them where the shots came from, and they turn toward Spencer. They lift their shot glasses in a cheers-in-appreciation gesture for buying them shots. They can only see the back of Jimmy's head and Spencer's face, so they don't know the shots came from their competition.

"Best of luck to you, gentlemen! Cheers!" Spencer yells. "Suckers," he whispers.

Carla delivers their food orders, and Spencer doesn't hesitate to enjoy his Rueben Fritters, but Jimmy doesn't touch his meal.

"What's wrong, brutha? You haven't touched your burger yet," Spencer asks.

"I can't eat, I'm too nervous. My stomach is in knots. I think I'm just going to head to the stadium and walk off these nerves," Jimmy answers.

"Hey bro, you've been preparing your whole life for this. You're the only guy I know who was a cheerleader for a Pop Warner team as a kid. You have dressed as the Notre Dame *Leprechaun* on Halloween for eight consecutive years. Don't even get me started on how you get the parties going every St. Patrick's Day. You fucking got this, bro!" Spencer says, to boost Jimmy's confidence.

"Thank you, Spence. And it's eleven years in a row, not eight," Jimmy replies.

Jimmy takes a few French fries and leaves his favorite booth. Spencer continues to enjoy his meal and Guinness.

"Good luck; I'm going to hang out here and have a drink or two or three with my new friends at the bar," Spencer says.

"You're going to get them too fucked up to participate," Jimmy says.

"That's the plan. And who knows, maybe one or both might be into a little extra fun. So, if you don't see me in the student section, I'm probably still here or in one of their dorm rooms," Spencer says.

Jimmy arrives at the stadium an hour before the Blue-Gold spring game begins and heads into the corridor leading to his locker room. He has to be on the field 30 minutes before the kickoff to start his final test to become the Notre Dame *Leprechaun*.

Jimmy enters the locker room, sees two other candidates preparing for the competition, and greets them with a nod. Jimmy sits in front of his locker and takes a deep breath before getting dressed in the iconic green suit and hat. One last glimpse into the mirror, he tells himself *You Got This!* He grabs his shillelagh stick and heads to the football field sidelines.

Jimmy and the other two finalists stand before the ten judges on the football sidelines. They're all dressed and ready for the final test… Get the fans cheering! LaTonya Jackson is looking around and then at her watch.

"Do any of you know where the other five of your group are? They're 10 minutes late. The stadium is filling up with fans, and it's time to kick off the excitement," LaTonya asks.

"Yeah, not a good start for them. Being on time and ready to go is an essential part of the *Leprechaun* legacy and shouldn't be taken lightly," adds former *Leprechaun* Nick Kacey, current judge and brother of the Miami Dolphins' star tight end Trevor Kacey.

Jimmy's looking around and needs clarification on why the other five have yet to appear. He thinks *this is a once-in-a-lifetime opportunity, and you're late*? However, he also thinks *I'm guaranteed a spot as a Leprechaun if they don't show.*

With only three positions awarded, the final test would determine which team you are with. The ultimate goal is to be the coveted Gold team and to help lead the football and basketball teams to victory. Of course, there are still other events and sports the Gold team has to do, but it's worth it for the grand prize of top *Leprechaun*. The Green team is the least desired option, and they are stuck cheering for the tennis and swim teams. However, no matter the team, it's still an iconic and honored position.

Julie finds Spencer in the student section and sits next to him. He's already watching Jimmy starting to warm up the crowd. They hug and join the Fighting Irish faithful in cheering.

"Your man is a natural out there. Did you get what you had to do accomplished?" Spencer shouts.

"Yes, did you get your job done?" she asked in return.

"Absolutely. Everything should be good, nothing to worry about," Spencer replies.

"How did you do it? I'm dying to know," Julie asks.

"I got them drunk, walked them back to their dorm room, and they passed out. I stayed long enough to ensure they don't wake up and return here in time for tryouts," he answers.

"Ahh, you mean you didn't kill them?" she responds with attitude.

"Kill them? We don't have to kill anyone. We're assigned to ensure he wins and help take out the competition. Wait, are you telling me you killed your assignments?" he says.

"Well, yes, I thought we had to do that. They said *take out the competition*!" she responds, defending her choice.

"No, you're not. With three of the eight finalists dying on the same day, everyone will suspect something now," he says condescendingly.

"Don't worry, they're all going to look like accidents or on purpose. Olivia took too many sleeping pills. The annoying douche bag, jock cheerleader guy will be found with a needle of heroin in his arm, and that quiet school shooter-looking son-of-a-bitch is lying in his bathtub filled with blood from his wrists," She reports.

"Two questions. First, did you cover your tracks, and it's not traceable to you? Two, where the fuck did you get heroin?" Spencer asks.

"Yes, I covered all my tracks. And Gary, Indiana, is only an hour away; finding some China White there wasn't hard," she answers.

They continue to watch Jimmy work the crowd and smile as they witness the making of Notre Dame's next Gold team, *Leprechaun*.

Monday morning has arrived, and it's the day that the judges will notify Jimmy of his *Leprechaun* tryout results. He feels great about his chances for the Gold team but doesn't want to jinx himself. He noticed a few mistakes the other finalists made. The news about the tragic loss of the 3 Notre Dame *Leprechaun* finalist has spread. The parents and conspiracy theorists are already calling for an investigation into foul play, but the authorities are satisfied with the conclusion of an O.D. and two suicides.

Jimmy and Spencer were hanging out in the dorm room and decided to skip their early class today to wait for the judges' email.

"It's 8:03 am, and they said they'll email the results at 8:00 am. What's the hold-up? Are they still trying to decide? That's it, I'm the fucking Green team!" Jimmy says while pacing around the room.

"Bro, chill. You got this; I have no doubt. The Gold team email will be delivered soon," Spencer says.

There's a knock on the door, and Jimmy thinks *they're delivering the news in person*. He opens the door, and it's Julie with a box of "Jack's Donuts" and iced coffees, just what he needs to help calm his nerves.

"Hey babe, any news yet?" she says, walking through the door and kissing Jimmy on the cheek.

"Not yet; they're now five minutes late. Thank you for the coffee and donuts. I'm hoping for that Gold team email, but I feel bad for those other five finalists. I can't believe three of them died, and thanks to Spencer, I already know what happened to the other two," he says, with a little hint of anger.

"Hey bro, it's not my fault they couldn't handle their liquor. Hell, one of them said he doesn't even want to be a fucking *Leprechaun*," Spencer defends himself.

"Well, I just hope this doesn't tarnish my win in the eyes of my dad and Grandpa. They might see it as me getting lucky that the other five didn't show up," he says.

Jimmy's cell phone starts to vibrate on his desk. This time, he thinks *I'm getting the news by phone*. He picks up the phone, and it displays Dad on the screen.

"Hey, Dad, how's it going? I don't have any news yet. It should be any minute now," he answers.

"Yes, you'll get the results in the next minute. I know you'll be happy. Welcome to the Gold team, *Leprechaun* fraternity son. Grandpa's here too," his dad says.

"Yeah, only because we had to knock off five of his competitors. What happened to the good ole days when you could buy off judges to ensure the right candidate is selected?" Patrick accidentally reveals.

"What's he talking about, Dad? What do you mean we had to knock off my competitors?" he asks.

"Don't mind your Grandpa, he's just talking shit like he normally does. We're just that confident in you," J.D. replies.

Suddenly, there is an email alert on his computer and cell phone titled "Welcome to the *Leprechaun* Gold Team." Jimmy, Spencer, and Julie jump up and down, cheering. The rest of the email is just details about assignments, what to expect, rules, and other bullshit he'll read through later. He immediately sends the acceptance email letter back.

"I told you, son, that you would win. Now, you're part of a proud tradition you'll carry forever. And next year, it will be your turn, Spencer. And Julie, you will be on the Gold team during your senior year," J.D. says.

"I still can't believe we allow gays, blacks, and chicks to become *Leprechauns*. I didn't vote on that, but I must embrace it. However, those tranny people are where I draw the line. Welcome to the group, Jimmy; well done. Spencer and Julie, good job doing your part. Except next time, don't kill anyone. That was a bitch to clean up!" Patrick says.

"What the fuck? Don't kill anyone? A bitch to clean up? What did you guys do?" Jimmy shouts.

"I'll explain everything to him, Mr. O'Sullivan. It'll be okay," Spencer says.

Jimmy hangs up the phone and looks at Julie and Spencer with confusion and anger. He doesn't understand what is happening, but he now knows they had something to do with the five finalists' failure to appear.

"Jimmy, This is something your dad and granddad were going to tell you over the summer. They have a presentation to show you, but I'll give you the basics. Try not to get pissed because this is a part of the tradition and has gone on for years. Your Grandpa and Dad started a secret society of *Leprechauns* called *The Green Suits*. They have influenced every decision on who the next Gold team *Leprechaun* is. *The Green Suits* don't care about the Blue and Green teams as much. They've bought off judges, caused other candidates to miss or fail the competition, and more recently killed other contenders," Spencer reveals, giving Julie a look.

"I can't believe this. So, I didn't earn the spot, it was fucking fixed? I don't want it this way," Jimmy says.

"Look, Jimmy, you don't have a choice. Every Gold leader since your granddad is a member of *The Green Suits*, and you can't change or fuck that up. Now, this year, we had a screw-up in communication, and some students had untimely deaths. That's past and can't be changed. Everyone you know and love, including the two of us, will be thrown in jail for life. This is a part of you now. So, you'll embrace it, help me and Julie win, and reap the benefits of becoming a *Green Suits* member and called a Notre Dame *Leprechaun*," Spencer says firmly.

"How did you guys get involved? I still don't completely understand your role in this. Did my family hire you?" Jimmy asks.

"Sort of. We are like you, Jimmy; we've wanted to be part of the Gold team of *Leprechauns* since childhood, that calling you can't ignore. My dad reached out to your father a year ago and asked him how I could become the *Leprechaun*; call it rich people's privilege. That's when they made a deal to help each other. So, our fathers arranged for us to be roommates. I will help you become the Gold team next year, and you'll help me in the same capacity for the year after that," Spencer explains.

"Pretty much the same story for me, except my Mom reached out to your dad. So, being a good catholic girl, loving Notre Dame my whole life, and hearing they were becoming more diverse with the *Leprechauns*, I had to become one. I met you on purpose, not by chance. However, everything I feel for you is real, and together, we could be the first Gold team *Leprechaun* couple and *Green Suit* members. We will help shape the future leaders of America by ensuring they become Gold team *Leprechauns*." Julie adds.

Jimmy is still a bit shocked and stands quietly for a few minutes. Julie and Spencer give him some time to process everything. Jimmy rereads the email's subject line... Welcome to the *Leprechaun* Gold Team. He smiles and looks at his two closest confidants.

"Fuck it! I'm a Gold team *Leprechaun*!" he shouts, giving them a group hug.

Spencer and Julie feel a sigh of relief at Jimmy's acceptance of the situation. They end their group embrace and are excited that the plan worked.

"Wait, one more question. Which one of you killed those students?" Jimmy asks.

"Yeah, that was my bad. I misunderstood the instructions to take out the competition," Julie says as she shrugs her shoulders, and they all laugh.

"Your first lesson as a Gold team winner, which your dad taught us, is *The Green Suits* motto... OLFL," Spencer says.

"Once a *Leprechaun*, Forever a *Leprechaun*!" Julie and Spencer say together.

TERMINAL LANCE

Mikey Piper has had little luck since his tour of duty ended for the United States Marines. He wasn't allowed to re-enlist for the 3rd time after his last 4-year stint as one of the few, the proud. He couldn't stay out of trouble and exited the Marines after finishing his 2nd commitment to service. After eight years in the Marine Corps, most Marines would be Sergeants, Staff Sergeants, or at the least a corporal by this point. Mikey's lack of ah... Marine standards, we'll call it, prevented him from promotions and any leadership responsibilities. He left the Marines as a Lance Corporal, or what they call a 'Terminal Lance.'

His actions and non-actions left the Marines with no choice but to refuse his re-enlistment. This rejection immediately led him to civilian life, which he wasn't ready for. Mikey has no family to speak of, and he lost touch with all his friends from back home years after he left for boot camp. Even during his eight years in the Marines, he burned many bridges: his best and only friend, Cpl. Roberto Robles can't take him in because his wife hates Mikey and doesn't want him freeloading around their house anymore. One day, he's on his 3-mile run, and the next day, he's on a city bus taking him out of Camp Pendleton for good. Mikey didn't have hardly any possessions, making it easier to carry everything in one sea bag.

That was about three years ago today. Mikey made his way to Phoenix, Arizona, not because of work, family, or a woman. He's been homeless since that day he saw Camp Pendleton for the last time out of the city bus window. Mikey could only partially adjust to civilian life. For example, he's frequently spotted talking to himself or doing something weird, even though he never took drugs or alcohol. He was just... Odd!

Becky and Scott Langston are pure outdoors people. They own cabins in Pine Top and Flagstaff, Arizona, and leave the city almost every weekend for one of these places to escape. Their weekday "9-5" job is the owner of a "Beers and Blades" knife and axe throwing bar in Scottsdale, Arizona. "B &

B," they call it for short, isn't the typical axe-throwing venue that most places are. They also have lanes to rent for throwing knives and Chinese stars. They're busy every night, except Mondays and Tuesdays when they are closed. The customers are groups of friends or families, corporate team builders, leagues, and regulars out for a good time. Their success has allowed them to live a lovely life with a beautiful home in Scottsdale and two cabins in the high country.

Becky oversees marketing, social media, day-to-day operations, and hiring. Scott handles alcohol, entertainment, equipment, and league nights. They're looking to open another location in the metro Phoenix area. They have one of the most popular entertainment establishments in Arizona.

The normal operations of "Beers and Blades" do extremely well financially. However, this differs from how Becky and Scott make the big bucks. They hold a secret event once a month on a late Monday night that brings in serious greenbacks. This special event is only for "V.I.P." clientele and requires each member's complete trust and confidentiality.

Mikey isn't having his best day walking around downtown Phoenix this evening. The July heat has him struggling to find a place to cool off. He often wonders why he left California, where Venice Beach was his backyard and the many perks the state gives people without housing. Such as free cell phones, health benefits, gym memberships just to shit and shower, numerous shelters and food banks, and $200 a month to spend. Then he remembers how cut-throat the homeless became with each other, constantly fighting over land, food, sex, and anything they could get their hands on for free. He called it "The Real Hunger Games".

A fellow homeless colleague told him how much less dangerous it was in Phoenix to be homeless if you could stand the heat for three months. Mikey said to himself, "Shit, if I can survive Marine desert training in 29 Palms, then Phoenix's summer heat would be like Club Med."

Only days and nights like this will he dream of that cool ocean breeze hitting his face. The worst thing that's happened to him so far in Phoenix is that a few Arizona State frat boys threw some beer on him after a Diamondbacks game last year.

One of the biggest concerns many Arizonians have is the rush of Californians relocating to the Grand Canyon state and changing the culture to match that of the Golden State. Mikey has the same fear with the potential of a homeless invasion. Right now, the Californian vagabonds have it made with all the free stuff given to them by the state, so many of them don't want to leave the California beaches. However, that could all change any day, and the new inhabitants arriving in Phoenix would cause new laws that would mirror California. These changes would bring a surge of vagrants to the valley of the sun, and it would be California all over again, just without the beautiful coastline. At this time, he walks around downtown Phoenix for a whole day and only sees a few dozen homeless people, but in California, they are everywhere.

"We have the same problem as the rich people," he laughs while thinking about the Californian rush.

"Don't California, my Arizona! Don't California, my Arizona!" he starts chanting out loud while walking down Washington Street, passing by people out on the town for the night.

"That's right, buddy. You tell those Californians to go back home." One of the men says to him mockingly while the group passes by and laughs.

Mikey pays them no attention; he's used to all the teasing and jokes. He also knows that everyone sees him as a drunk or meth head because he's homeless, even though he never touches any of that "brain junk." They don't realize that Mikey is very aware of his surroundings; he's just dirty and stinks.

Becky and Scott aren't just successful business owners, respected residents of Scottsdale, and socially popular. They're also highly charitable. Becky has a charity for abused women and holds fund-raising events where these women get to throw axes at giant pictures of their abuser's head. Depending on where the axe hits the target determines the amount people donate... Right between the eyes is $1,000!

Scott spends a lot of time trying to prevent animal cruelty. He also sponsors an event at "Beers and Blades" four times a year to help support his cause. He calls this event "Axes for Animals" or "A4A" for short. "A4A" is a competition for the best axe throwers to win prize money and a trophy. This special event has become so popular that ESPN 3 airs it. Besides the prize fund, all proceeds go towards his animal cruelty charity.

One thing that Becky and Scott do together to be more charitable is something they like to keep to themselves. Once a month, they find six willing homeless people to join them at "Beers and Blades" for a nice dinner, a chance to shower, and provide new clothes for them. After finishing that, they let the less fortunate throw axes and knives before returning them to the streets.

Mikey continues his stroll down the less busy streets of downtown Phoenix in search of a place to sleep for the evening. One of his usual go-to locations is an alley tucked away from Adams Street that is homeless-free. The business owners who share the alley are accepting of his presence. Mikey's well-liked because he doesn't bother customers by begging, stays out of the way, and is friendly with the staff. Last year, a few of the restaurant's waitstaff banded together and donated some tips to get Mikey a hotel room for a weekend. The main reason the business owners like him around is because they know he wouldn't allow anyone to break in. Mikey used his Marine training and thwarted two burglary attempts just last month by chasing off the culprits. The businesses, primarily restaurants, gladly feed him in exchange for the free home(less) security.

Mikey pulls out a few items from his trusted Fry's shopping cart, which he's had for nearly a year. The front left wheel on the cart probably has another month left, so he knows he'll have to exchange it for a new cart. He makes a nice bed by a dumpster with some old blankets and lays down to sleep.

Becky pulls the big black passenger van into the alley and parks it behind one of the businesses closed for the night. Scott exits the van and walks over to where Mikey is lying down.

"Excuse me, sir. My name is Scott, and I'd like to offer you a free dinner, shower, and set of clothes. Afterward, if you come with us now, a free night of axe-throwing fun at our 'Beers and Blades' location." Scott asks in a calm and friendly tone.

Mikey sits up and looks at Scott's van, which he's invited him to enter. He sees the "Beers and Blades" name and logo in big yellow letters on the side of the van. All the windows are tinted, so he can't determine who's inside.

"You want me to get into the big dark van and leave with you and whoever is driving?" He asks curiously.

"Yes, sir, once a month, we provide an evening of food, clothes, and fun for the less fortunate like yourself. We know it's not a solution to your problems, but it may give you hope for better things." Scott replies.

"Well, usually when something is too good, it's too good. I think I'll stay here in what I like to call my mobile home." Mikey says.

"I promise you, sir, there is no catch, no gimmicks, and we will return you to this very spot at the end of the night." Scott pleads.

"Why me? Plenty of homeless people would love to take you up on this wonderful, suspicious offer," he asks.

"Good question. We have five others already in the van. As I mentioned, we do this once a month for six homeless people at a time. Our only requirement is that you have fun!" Scott answers.

"If you promise to return me to my stuff tonight and everything you say is true, I will gladly accept your offer. What's on the menu?" Mikey accepts.

"That's great. Tonight, you'll have a delicious cheeseburger and fries from the locally famous Chef Adam Allister, a champion on Fox's Sliced and Diced cooking show," Scott answers.

"Never heard of him," Mikey replies.

Mikey gathers all of his belongings and places them behind a dumpster for safekeeping until his return. He follows Scott to the van and enters through the sliding side door. He sees the other five lucky homeless people and Becky behind the wheel, waiting for him to board and sit.

"Welcome, sir. What's your name?" Becky asks.

"It's Mikey Piper," he answers.

"It's nice to meet you, Mikey. Please take your seat, and we will be off to Beers and Blades," Becky requests.

Scott climbs into the front passenger seat and turns on the radio, playing "Hotel California" by the Eagles. Mikey rolls his eyes in disgust, he *really fucking hates this song.* Becky drives the van and begins their 30-minute trip to "Beers and Blades" in Scottsdale.

The parking lot is empty, and the street is relatively quiet with traffic. Becky pulls around to the back of the building, where two nice cars are parked. Becky stops the van close to the rear entrance, allowing Mikey and his fellow homeless companions to climb out of the van. Scott gets out of the passenger's seat and unlocks the back door. They enter "Beers and Blades," and the inside is much bigger than Mikey had imagined. They walk down a short hallway, and Scott guides them into an employee break room.

"Okay, friends, in those boxes on the table are new clothes for men and women. You will find jeans, t-shirts, socks, underwear, and many more items. Grab what you want to change into and take it to the men's and women's showers here in the backrooms," Scott instructs.

The small group of homeless, except Mikey, rush over to the boxes and begin rummaging through them in search of something to wear. Mikey slowly and casually walks over and grabs some jeans that fit him and a large T-shirt with A.S.U. Sun Devils on the front.

After about 15 minutes of everyone getting a chance to shower and get dressed, the three homeless men and three homeless women meet back in the break room. Mikey slips on his new Fila tennis shoes and walks out of the bathroom. He's the last one to arrive in the breakroom. Everyone is sitting at the table drinking a beer and eating snacks Becky brought them. Suddenly, a man enters through the breakroom door just a minute after Mikey did. He has a tray of cheeseburgers and a large bowl of French fries.

"Hello, everyone. I'm the locally famous Chef Adam Allister. I have prepared my signature burger, 'Excalibeef,' for you. It consists of seasoning, pepperjack cheese, bacon, lettuce, tomato, and my special blended secret sauce. It is accompanied by our tasty French fries. Please enjoy, I'm Chef Adam!" He says as he takes a bow and dramatically exits.

The homeless crew grab a burger and pile some fries on their plate from the giant metal bowl. Everyone eats frantically, but Mikey takes his time and savors the flavors. Bill Simmons, or as he's known on the streets, Crazy Billy, is the first to finish. Unless you count scraps from *Majerle's Sports Grill's* dumpster, he hasn't had a good meal all month. Sally Ward, who Mikey believes gave him crabs last month, is the next to finish and runs to the bathroom. Mikey says, "Most likely to pick those little creepy crawlers out of her pubic hair forest."

Mikey decides he's had enough after the thought of Sally's crab-infested snatch. He pushes aside the remaining leftovers and walks around to settle his stomach.

"You're not going to finish that burger?" Dirty Dan Hillman asks, already sliding the plate over in his direction.

"All yours, buddy," Mikey replies.

"Didn't you enjoy the selection of burgers locally famous Chef Adam prepared for you, sir? I'm Chef Adam!" The chef asks, suddenly and silently appearing behind Mikey.

"Holy fuck, you scared the shit out of me, man," Mikey says, startled.

"My apologies, sir. Locally famous Chef Adam just noticed you didn't eat all of your burger and needed to understand why? I'm Chef Adam!" Chef replies.

"I did enjoy it, chef. Possibly one of the best burgers I've had. I just lost my appetite and needed to walk around a bit. I appreciate the food, thank you," he replies,

Locally famous Chef Adam nods and returns to the kitchen, staring at Mikey the whole time. The remaining homeless finish their meals and beer. Becky enters the breakroom and asks them to be all seated. Sally returns from the bathroom and sits next to Mikey. He gets up and moves to the other side of the table. She lets him know she was insulted with a dirty look.

"I'm so glad you all agreed to spend the evening with us here at 'Beer and Blades.' I hope you enjoyed locally famous Chef Adam's burgers?" Becky asks.

"They were delicious. I had mine, and half of that dude's right there. I also ate that weird fucker's burger over there. He's too busy swatting at flies that don't exist," Dirty Dan confesses.

Becky looks annoyed at him for admitting he ate burgers that weren't his but quickly moves on.

"In about 15 minutes, after Scott finishes setting up the throwing lanes, we will take you to the axe and knife throwing area for you guys to enjoy an hour of blade-throwing fun. Then we will return you safely to where we picked you up," Becky explains.

"I've never thrown an axe or knife before. Doesn't sound like that much fun to me," Isla Vasquez says with a heavy Spanish accent.

"We will show you how before you start. It's easy, and once you get the correct throwing technique, it's a blast," Becky answers.

"Do we get more beer?" Dirty Dan asks.

"Absolutely. I'll be back to get you in just a few minutes," Becky says as she leaves the breakroom.

Mikey continues to pace around the breakroom. He's beginning to feel uneasy about what's going on. The rest of the group sits at the table, picking at the remaining fries and snacks, except for the mystery homeless man, who is killing all the flies buzzing around his head. He doesn't speak, and nobody knows his name.

Mikey's suspicions grow, and he decides to investigate the throwing areas at the front of "Beer and Blades," where Becky and Scott are. He walks down the long hallway, passing the bathroom, kitchen, and closet doors. He reaches the main area and peeks in but doesn't see Becky, Scott, or anyone. The whole front end of the building is quiet. Mikey begins walking back to the breakroom but peeks into the kitchen first. Locally famous Chef Adam Allister seems to be preparing more meals, but he is alone. Mikey thinks to himself, *they are feeding us well*.

He approaches the breakroom door and opens it. He sees that all his fellow homeless companions, except the bug-swatting mystery man, are passed out on the floor and table.

Suddenly, Becky comes through a door toward the back of the building near the rear exit they came in through earlier. He looks at her but starts to feel a bit dizzy at the same time. He reaches for the door frame to hold himself up.

"What are you doing out here, and why aren't you asleep?" she asks, a bit surprised to see Mikey standing there.

"What's going on? Why is every one asleep, and I feel dizzy?" Mikey replies as he slowly falls to his knees.

"Well, you were supposed to eat all your burger, then you would be asleep already. No worries, you should be out in a few more seconds. We drugged your burgers with Rohypnol so that you won't feel a thing later," Becky admits.

"You fucking roofied us? And what do you mean we won't feel anything? You motherfu…." Mikey says before completely passing out.

Scott is finishing tying Mikey up to the wooden axe-throwing target board. Becky approaches him from the small crowd, enjoying beers in the common area at the center of the room, to converse with him privately.

"Scott, a couple of issues that locally famous Chef Adam and I had to deal with. First, one of the vagrants died from a roofie O.D. He ate 2 ½ burgers. We still tied him up; they won't be able to tell he's already dead. Second, one didn't eat, so locally famous Chef Adam had to crack him over the head with a meat tenderizer a few times to knock him out. Lastly, this piece of shit vagabond you're tying up now didn't eat that much and barely passed out," Becky reports.

"No worries, you and locally famous… Do we really have to keep calling him that?" Scott replies, getting annoyed.

"Yeah, it's in his contract I agreed to. I immediately regretted my decision," Becky answers.

"Ugh, well, like you said, the clients won't know the status of these fucking bums. Hopefully, this one will stay passed out long enough to get an axe through his skull," Scott replies, slapping Mikey over the head.

The 12 clients sit at the tables in the lounge area of the private axe-throwing room in "Beers and Blades." The room has three throwing lanes on each side, a lounge in the middle, and a bar on the far wall. The opposite wall has the exit door leading to the secret entrance for special guests only. Becky and Scott stand in front of the group and address them.

"Welcome to 'Hatchet the Homeless' everyone. It is great to see new faces and a few returning ones. Hello Sal," Becky greets with a welcoming but also sinister smile.

"As you know, your entry fee of $25,000 will get you beer, food by locally famous Chef Adam Allister, and one hour of throwing axes or knives at the ah, less fortunate, we'll call them. The winner of this evening's contest gets one free entry to the next 'Hatchet the Homeless,' like Mr. Sal Sanderson, brother of the billionaire Sid Sanderson," Scott says while pointing at a middle-aged man with long hair and a beard who's snorting a line of coke on the table.

Sal waves to everyone while wiping his nose after his cocaine intake with his other arm. The others look over but aren't impressed. They all know of his troublemaking past from the tabloids. Sid gives him a monthly allowance and bought him a house in Phoenix so he can stay out of the way. He uses most of that money to party, travel, fuck women and men, and kill homeless people a few times a year. He's a "Hatchet the Homeless" regular.

"Using only axes and knives, the scoring is as follows: 10 points for headshots, 8 points for chest, 5 points for groin area, and 1 point for any other body part. We will have five rounds, with everyone paired up at each throwing zone. If at the end of all five rounds, your target is still alive because you suck, then you will have a $5,000 fine, and everyone else gets to throw at the target," Scott explains.

"Excellent. That said, let's get to it and 'Hatchet the Homeless'!" Becky shouts with excitement.

The 12 contestants cheered and took a position in their assigned throwing lane. The group had come to the regular

"Beers and Blades" hours earlier in the week to practice and learn how to throw the axe and knife properly. Becky and Scott looked at each group and announced that round one had begun. Each contestant would intermittently throw three axes and three knives until everyone was done throwing. Scott and Becky would officially verify all scoring for the round.

In Lane One, Brice Baker, a local T.V. news reporter, is throwing against his best friend and local network producer, Chance Lewis. They're both pretty shit-faced and giggling like school girls. Chance throws first and completely misses their target... Crazy Billy.

Over in Lane Two, there is a battle of famous female besties and competitors, the entertainment mogul Odelia Winfred and music diva Madam Gigi. Odelia throws first and strikes Sally Ward in the leg, but the axe doesn't stick. She remains passed out and doesn't feel it.

The remaining lanes are occupied by wealthy business owners around town, Sal Sanderson and a mystery man wearing shades, nice clothes, and a hat. Because of the high-profile clients that come here, every client signs a non-disclosure agreement, and no cell phones or cameras are allowed. They know that if the "Code of Silence" is broken, they may one day end up on the opposite end of the axe-throwing lane.

Two nicely dressed businessmen are taking turns throwing and missing. Mikey doesn't hear the banging of steel around his head. One of the knives, the wrong end, even struck him in the shoulder, and he didn't budge. The smaller dose of the drug must have been good enough.

"YES!" a loud cheer comes over from Lane One. Brice Baker has a perfect hit to Crazy Billy's head. The axe is wedged in his face and is an instant kill shot—10 points for Brice.

Everyone else quickly takes their final turns and rushes over to Lane One to view the gory axe wound to Crazy Billy's cranium. Meanwhile, Becky and Scott take one side each to tally up the points after round one. Crazy Billy just has one headshot, and Sally Ward has two knives in her torso and an axe in her leg. Dirty Dan, who was already dead, had an axe in his shoulder, his right hand, and one that clipped his leg. The businessmen in

Lane Four show off their accuracy and blade-throwing skills with two axes and three knives throughout his chest and stomach, killing the unknown fly-swatting homeless man.

Becky approaches Lane Six, where Sal and the nicely dressed mystery man are. She walks over to their target, Mikey Piper, to count their score.

"Nothing? Did you guys both miss the target on all 12 shots combined? That's a first. I've had special needs kids throw better than you," Becky smack-talks to them.

They both bow their heads in shame as the rest of the group laugh at them. Scott and Becky walk back to the center to announce the scores.

"Okay, Lane Four is in the lead with 18 points and an extra 2 points for the kill shot, for 20 points. Lane One is in 2nd place with a headshot and a kill shot for 12 total points. Lane Two, The Divas, as they want to be referred, has 10 points, including kill shot points. So, three of the six targets remain alive. Let's start round two in ten minutes. Thank you," Scotts reports.

Round two begins after the group enjoyed another beer, mini chimichangas, fried mozzarella sticks, and bathroom breaks. After some friendly smack talk and laughter, the groups return to their throwing lanes. The extra beers during break didn't help their aims. Becky and Scott report the scores after the 2nd round. Lane Four is way ahead with 32 points, and one more lane scores a kill shot. Lane Six scores zero points for the second time in a row. The group is harassing them with insults and finger-pointing, which annoys Sal. He's now determined to score big in round 3. This leaves only Isla Vasquez and Mikey Piper still alive. However, Isla has a few knife wounds through her arms, shoulders, and legs.

After another ten-minute break, round three begins. The next round of beer and food has these V.I.P.s aiming poorly with full stomachs and a drunken buzz. Sal is on his 2nd axe throw this round. He focuses while swaying from the drugs and beer. He lifts the axe and throws it in Mikey's direction. The axe clips the top of Mikey's shoulder and cuts him. The feel of the axe's blade startles him awake from the sharp pain. He quickly scans the area, realizes he's tied up, and glances at Sal and the Unknown Man. Sal panics and throws a knife at him. Mikey lifts his tied-up left arm towards his face but only makes it a few inches. The knife strikes the rope and cuts through half of it. Mikey notices this and starts pulling hard, ripping the rope from his left arm. The mystery man screeches like a 10-year-old and points at Mikey getting loose.

Becky comes running over to see what's going on. The two young rich douchey guys in Lane Three, probably trust fund babies, turn around to see what is happening across from them in Lane Six. Mikey quickly unties himself and is free. He grabs one of the axes lying on the floor at his feet. Sal throws his last knife, and Mikey blocks it with the axe.

Mikey charges at the group of people, like a Marine storming the beaches of Iwo Jima. Sal pushes the mystery man in Mikey's direction. A swift strike severs the man's head, and it rolls in front of the douchey guys in Lane Three. The shades and hat fall off the rolling head.

"Holy shit, that's World-Famous Author Lance Hyden. I knew that dude had to be famous," one of the young douchey men states.

Becky grabs an axe and starts a swinging battle with Mikey. She misses, and Mikey strikes down on her shoulder. She screams in agony. The two douchebags throw knives at Mikey but miss by a mile.

Madam Gigi runs to the exit, still carrying her axe. She trips and falls perfectly on the axe's blade, slicing her face and head in half, and her body is now blocking the exit. Odelia Winfred is puking all over Lane Two from witnessing her best friend's face in two locations.

Mikey reaches the douchebags, and they try and fight him off. They fail, and Mikey ends them both in a gory, horrific fashion. Brice and Chance are frantically trying to move Madam Gigi's body out of the way to exit. Sal reaches the exit first and tries to open the door by repeatedly bludgeoning Madam Gigi's head.

Mikey picks up two knives and rapidly slings them in the direction of Lane Four, instantly landing the blades into the skulls of the two businessmen.

Brice and Chance finally get Madam Gigi's lifeless body over enough to open the door all the way. One of the rich middle-aged men from Lane Five pushes Sal out of the way and quickly opens the door. A meat cleaver meets him to the face by locally famous Chef Adam Allister, who came running from the kitchen to help and panicked when the door opened. Per "Hatchet the Homeless" protocol, he quickly grabs the door, slams it shut, and locks it to avoid any escape by the homeless and running to the police. Brice tries to open it from the other side but is no match for the locked door. Chance joins in to add muscle power, but that doesn't help.

"Open the fucking door, chef! Let us out!" Brice yells.

"Not until I hear the 'All Clear' from Becky or Scott. I'm Chef Adam!" He yells back.

Mikey is approaching the other middle-aged man from Lane Five, and he quickly feels a knife penetrate his right arm. Scott was hiding in Lane Two and waiting for the right time to strike. Mikey pulls the knife out and throws it back at Scott. He misses and hits the puking Odelia Winfred in the neck. She pulls the knife out, and blood sprays all over Scott and Sally Ward. The talk show diva is panicking and running around in circles, desperately trying to hold the blood in with her hands. Scott grabs an axe out of Sally's stomach and trips Odelia. He splits her head open with the axe to put her out of misery but mostly to end that ear-piercing scream.

Mikey has dispatched the other middle-aged rich guy from Lane Five with his axe at the same time Scott's axe was finding Odelia's head. The two men stare at each other from opposite lanes across from each other. They both yell out and run at each other, like in a battle scene from "Braveheart."

While Brice and Chance are still pulling on the door to open it, Sal grabs Madam Gigi and one of the middle-aged businessmen's bodies, buries himself under them, and pretends to be dead.

After a couple of minutes of fighting, Mikey emerges from Lane Two, bloodied by the knife sticking out of his right leg and a couple axe slashes to his torso. His axe is dripping with Scott's blood and entrails hanging from it.

"Nooooo!" a scream from Becky, who is staggering towards him with an axe she can barely yield in her right hand.

Mikey almost feels sorry for her as she slowly swings the axe at him. Her wild swing and weak arm cause the axe to stick into her leg, and she screams in pain again. Mikey pauses a moment out of respect and then violently swings the axe and severs her head. Her headless body falls perfectly in place to where World Famous Author Lance Hyden's head is on the floor, making it appear as if his head is on her body. Mikey couldn't hold back his laughter at the newly formed dead person.

Brice suddenly stops pulling on the door and stands there. Chance continues to struggle and feels he's now the only one trying to open the door.

"What the fuck, Brice? Keep pulling, damn it," Chance yells.

Chance looks back at Brice and notices an axe sticking out of the back of his head, then quickly ripped out as brain matter flies onto his face. Brice's body takes a few seconds to fall to the ground, and Chance begins to plead for his life.

"Please, buddy, don't kill me. I'll pay you a lot of money. You wouldn't have to be homeless anymore," he begs, but it doesn't work.

Mikey chops him in half with a few blows, like the Ponderosa pine trees he used to cut down during his homeless time living in the high country. The top half of Chance's body lands on Sal's dead body's hiding place, helping to cover him up some more.

Mikey walks over the wall next to the door and silently and patiently waits until locally famous Chef Adam Allister opens the door. After a few minutes of silence, the chef seeks answers.

"Are you guys okay in there? Is anybody still alive? Who's there? I'm Chef Adam!" he yells, but there is still no sound.

He slowly opens the door and sees the carnage in the middle of the room. Blood and bodies are everywhere. He creeps into the room, and out of the corner of his eye, he sees Mikey swinging the axe in his direction.

"Ahh fuck, I'm Chef Ad…." He tries to yell out, but the axe perfectly connects with his open mouth and slices off the top half of his head in one mighty swing like a juicy, ripe tomato.

"They were right; he is champion of 'Sliced and Diced.'" Mikey quips.

Mikey drops the axe and looks over the room, taking in everything that happened. What lasted about ten minutes felt like hours. He's exhausted and sits at one of the tables, grabs a mozzarella stick, and eats it. He grabs one of the half-full beers and guzzles that down.

After a few more bites of food, the Marine finally gets up and walks towards the exit. He knows he will have a long walk back to his belongings in downtown Phoenix, so being covered in blood wouldn't be the best idea. He plans to stop in the breakroom, grab some more clothes, and shower.

"Don't worry, I'm not going to kill you. According to how you spend your life, Sal," Mikey says, " somebody or you will eventually do that for me, knowing exactly who and where the man is.

"Thank you!" in a muffled voice from the bodies covering him.

Mikey leaves the room to get cleaned up, and Sal stays there until he knows it's safe to leave. He's not going to the cops and knows Mikey isn't either. There are no cameras in the room or at this secret entrance. Mikey will wipe off the fingerprints of the axes and knives he used.

One "Beer and Blades" employee enters the back door to start their shift the following day. He notices the secret room employees were never allowed to enter is open. Blood, guts, bodies, and weapons lay everywhere. The employee pulls out his cell phone and calls 911.

"911. What's your emergency?" the operator asks.

"Yeah, it's like the Red Wedding from Game of Thrones here at 'Beer and Blades.' Please send the police, ambulance, and coroner," he requests.

10-PIN

Something must be said about watching a rotating shiny ball traveling down a well-oiled, layered 60-foot wooden lane towards the 10 defenseless bowling pins standing there like a herd of unsuspecting sheep. The thrill and anticipation that the ball you just released from the three-fingered drilled holes will strike down all 10 pins at once, or if any of those white statues will remain mocking you until your 2nd chance to mow them all down.

Bowling is one of America's most competitive and popular sports, with nearly 70 million people visiting a local bowling center at least once a year. Bowling alleys generate almost 25% of their yearly revenue from league nights. Men's, women's, co-ed, and kid leagues are at practically every bowling center in the country. The main draw of these leagues is meeting up once a week to compete against other teams, socialize, and enjoy an evening out for a couple of hours.

For one 5-member co-ed team that calls itself the "X-Men," there is a different calling to continue their league championship dominance in Phoenix, Arizona. They will have the opportunity to move on to regionals for a shot at being selected for Team USA at the 2028 Olympics.

For the first time ever, the Olympic committee has voted to include bowling as a summer Olympic sport, making its debut at the 2028 Olympics in Los Angeles, California. League champions across the country will get the opportunity to compete in the regional tournaments to earn their way to the national championship for the potential to represent the USA and go for gold. There will be several bowling categories in the Olympics: Men's team, Women's team, Mixed team, and finally, men's and women's singles. If the "X-Men" win their league championship, they will compete for only one of two mixed-team spots on Team USA.

Brothers Billy "Ace" and Bobby "Bob-A-Louie" Hayden have been bowling since they were young. Their father, Earl Hayden, was a professional bowler and 5-time PBA champion, meaning that Billy and Bobby were practically raised in bowling alleys. Neither brother would ever join the PBA due to life and family responsibilities, but they could give the pros a run for their money. League nights are sacred to the Brothers Hayden. This is where they've met most of their friends, Bobby found his wife, and it provides a getaway from the everyday grind of their careers.

Bobby's wife, Margo Hayden, is also a member of the "X-men" and the team's loudest and most supportive member. Her skills on the lanes are unmatched by most women in the league, except her teammate, Mona Greenwood, also known as the "White Pin Assassin," or "WPA" for short. Mona is a lethal lefty with her bright pink 14-pound bowling ball, and she's even more dangerous with her terrifying attitude. Her toughness is intimidating and keeps most of the single and some of the married men in the league from flirting with her. The final member of the "X-men" is Bruce "Bedposts" Wilkens. He's the youngest member and is very skilled in two areas of the bowling league night. First, picking up the nearly impossible and dreaded 7-10 split, also known as "bedposts" in the bowling world. Second, picking up women that he rates 7-10 on his "hotness" scale. These talents earned him the nickname "Bedposts" to honor his artistry in both categories.

In previous years, the objective was to win the league championship for the prize fund and bragging rights. Something the "X-Men" are very good at, winning 4 of the last 5 league seasons. The team's name was created by Bobby because of his love for collecting Marvel comic books, specifically his favorite, the *X-Men*. Since the X in bowling is a symbol for a strike, it was an obvious choice. He provided each team member with T-shirts of the *X-Men* comic book characters to match their persona. Bobby's shirt is *Professor X*, the leader of the *X-Men.* For his seriousness, laser focus, and competitive nature, he selected *Cyclops* for Billy. The perfect fit for Margo, with her fiery and outgoing demeanor, is *Storm*. Even though the comic character is male, Mona was given *Wolverine*, and she's okay with that. Finally, the good-looking playboy Bruce was anointed *Gambit*.

The "X-Men" is the most feared team at the "Bowl-A-Frama" in Phoenix, Arizona.

Every member of the "X-Men" is averaging over 200 for this season. They know it will take their best efforts tonight to win and advance to the regionals in two months. They currently own 1st place by two points, and the only team with a shot at beating them is their arch-rivals, team "neXt!!!". They currently sit in 2nd place and are their final opponent of the season.

Team "neXt!!!" consists of five siblings, three males and two females, who are arrogant and constant trash talkers. Most of the teams scheduled against them for that week know it will not be a fun night with their loud mouths and overwhelming team camaraderie for all three games.

One time, team "Spare Balls" was scheduled to play them, and every member sent a substitute to play for them so they didn't have to endure the agony of being on the same lanes for three hours with the team "neXt!!!" The league committee agreed that isn't allowed, warned all the teams, and awarded all four points of the match to the team "neXt!!!", which they had already won. The siblings constantly complained about it every week for two months until they finally let it die.

Most league teams are canceling their final matches this evening to watch the battle for "Bowl-A-Frama" supremacy and the chance to "Go for the Gold" in the 2028 Olympics. There will obviously be a heavily lopsided support for the "X-Men" tonight. The bowling alley decided to bring in some bleachers for the teams to sit on and watch from behind. The atmosphere was electric and tense as people began to arrive and find somewhere to watch lanes 23 and 24.

Team "neXt!!!" was already in their lanes and ready to go. They arrived at the bowling alley two hours ago to prepare themselves.

"Let's Go! Team neXt!!! We got this!" Jack "Hammer" Reynolds yells to motivate his teammates.

"*X-Men* are about to become the weak-ass *Justice League* after tonight. Los Angeles, here we come!" Johnny Reynolds responds.

"What does that even mean, bro? *The Justice League* has *Superman*, *Batman*, *Aquaman*, and *Wonder Woman*. They weren't weak at all. In fact, they were probably more powerful than the *X-Men*, one could argue," Jacqueline "Jackie" Reynolds states.

"Are you fucking crazy, sis? The *X-Men* would waste the *Justice League*. *D*C superheroes are much weaker than *Marvel*. Everybody knows that," Johnny Reynolds snaps back.

"I'm just saying it would be a good fight, and I think the *Justice League* might have the edge," Jackie eggs Johnny on.

"The *Justice League* also has the *Wonder Twins*," Johnny points out.

"Damn, great point. Yeah, *X-Men* are stronger," Jackie agrees.

The "X-Men" arrive at the "Bowl-A-Frama" and meet in the parking lot. Bobby and Margo are standing at the entrance, watching Billy and Mona walking towards them. They see Bruce ride up on this sleek black Harley... You didn't expect he'd be driving anything else, did you?

The team assembles before entering the bowling alley to face their nemesis and rivals, team "neXt!!!" They form a circle with arms around each other and lean into the center, looking downwards.

"May the bowling Gods give us the strength and power to be victorious. Let the pins fall to the ground like autumn leaves after they've browned. Let tonight be the first step toward the road to glory and gold. We will be victorious! 'X-Men' Unite!" Billy delivers the team prayer.

"Look, guys, don't let their annoying smack talk get under our skins. Keep bowling like we have all year, and they will not take three points from us," Bobby follows up with leadership.

"Yeah, fuck those mother fuckers!" Mona or Wolverine, whichever one that was, yells out.

"Hey, but you guys are still cool if I ask out Jackie Reynolds after the match, right?" Bruce asks.

They just stare at him and shake their heads. Bobby waves the team towards the bowling alley front doors to commence battle on the maplewood floors of the "Bowl-A-Frama." They enter the building one at a time in a single file, and I swear they are moving in slow motion. Margo's hair was blowing from the wind that followed them in. Mona flips off a kid who yells, "Go team neXt!!!". Bruce is giving all the ladies a smile and a wink. Bobby is leading the way and waving to his friends and "fans for the day." Billy is highly focused and doesn't acknowledge anybody around him, as he is already in a zone. Team "X-Men" has arrived.

"Are you guys trying to be a Tarantino movie with that entrance? Sit the fuck down and put on your bowling shoes, so we can get this beat down over with," Jeremy Reynolds, the most obnoxious and unpleasant member of their team, says.

Bobby had no clue what that reference was but ignored it and continued smiling and waving at everyone. Mona grabbed a man's beer can from his hand and was about to throw it at Jeremy, but Bruce grabbed her arm before hurling it. He retrieved the beer and returned it to the shocked man, who was just staring at Mona with fear. Billy walks over to the bowling center counter to rent his bowling shoes. All serious bowlers have their own shoes, but not Billy. He has never bought his own pair due to superstitious reasons.

He was bowling in an amateur event during his senior year in high school, and he was one pin away on his last roll in the tenth frame from bowling his first and only 300 game. The 10-pin just wobbled but never fell. Even though he would go on to win the event, he left disappointed by that 10-pin. Bobby, 2 years older than him, would give him the nickname "Ace" to mock him for missing that last pin. Of course, it was out of love, as brothers would do. Billy returned to that bowling alley later that night and asked the manager to give him that 10-pin from lane 24. He still has it to remind him how close he came to perfection. Something that he strives for every time he steps on to those lanes.

Billy approaches the counter, but nobody is in sight. He hopes the bowling alley's manager, Stella Kozlov, is behind the register to assist him. He's had a crush on Stella for a year, but he usually can only muster up an awkward schoolboy comment.

The serious competitor and league's best bowler has met his match with the gorgeous Russian woman who greets him weekly.

Suddenly, Peter "Huffing" Phillips pops up from behind the counter. He startles Billy for a second.

"How can I help ya, Billy? Anything you need to beat those poopholes?" he asks.

Billy is even more disappointed that he got help from "Huffing" Phillips, I mean Peter. He creeps mostly everyone out. He's why even the bowlers who don't take the league that seriously bought their own shoes instead of renting them. He's been caught a few times huffing the rental shoes of ladies who just finished bowling. He was homeless a year ago until he saved Stella's life one day, and she got him a job at the bowling alley where he also lives. They made him a small bedroom in the back of the lanes, where nobody could see.

"Just need your best size 9s Huf... Peter," Billy replies with fake enthusiasm.

"Comin' right up, Billy, our luckiest and cleanest pair. I've actually had them specially prepared for you, Billy. Nobody's worn these all week. I cleaned them out and polished them up. And you can call me 'Huffing.' I like it," he admits.

"Oh wow, that's pretty awesome 'Huffing.' Thank you for doing that," Billy replies, now thinking for the first time of finally buying his shoes.

He takes the shoes, quickly walks away from the front desk, and "Huffing" Phillips. He quickly glances back and sees "Huffing" smiling and waving. This means that when Billy wasn't looking at him, he was still smiling and waving. That creeped Billy out even more.

Billy focuses on lanes 23 and 24 a few yards ahead and doesn't look back again. "Huffing" returns to the shoe rental rack and huffs women's shoes; size 7 is his preference.

The two teams are making final preparations for the first game. Everyone can feel the tension in the air. Team "neXt!!!" is quiet for the first time all season. Bobby leans over to Billy.

"You hear that 'Ace'?" Bobby asks.

"Hear what? It's so quiet in here I can still hear Peter huffing shoes," Bobby responds.

"Exactly! They're not saying a word or talking shit. They're scared, bro." Bobby points out.

Bruce smiles confidently while staring Jeremy right in the eye from across the scorer's table.

"What the fuck are you smiling at Gambit, or Bambit, or lame bit? He's the weakest of the Avengers anyway, dumb ass." Jeremy says, and people laugh at his superhero ignorance.

"Dude, shut up! You don't even know what you're talking about, so your trash talk only makes you look stupid," Johnny whispers to his brother.

"What are you talking about, bro? I just comedy central roasted his ass," Jeremy replies while giggling at his own comic book reference.

"Gambit was an 'X-Men, not an avenger. You know, like their team's name, 'X-Men.' Get it? You fucking idiot," Johnny sarcastically replies back.

"Whatever, Johnny, 'X-Men, Avenger, Justice League, who gives a fuck? We're going to crush them," Jeremy says, getting riled up and bringing the team "neXt!!!" that nobody "loves" back.

"Next! Next! Next!" the team chants while starting their practice round, and almost everyone in the crowd rolls their eyes.

The match begins as Margo and Jackie bowl first for their respective teams. Margo only needs one ball to knock down all her 10 pins; Jackie needs a 2nd ball. The crowd cheers for Margo's strike. Bruce bowls next and joins his team mate in the strike category. In fact, all five members of "X-Men" bowled a strike in the first frame. This briefly silenced their rivals until Jack "Hammer" struts up to his mark. Despite his team's annoying arrogance, the ladies love watching Jack "Hammer" Reynolds bowl. He could give Bruce a run for his money with all the ladies, but he is gay. He bowls a strike, and his team cheers excessively loud to purposely be annoying.

Bobby approaches the pins in the 6th frame and throws a perfect strike. Besides, Billy, that was the only strike for both teams in that rough frame.

"Woo, Woo. That's my Poopsie-Dingy!" Margo would yell with her signature Woo Woo shout.

"Way to go, Bob-A-Louie!" Bruce, who's like a son to Bobby, shouts.

In the 8th frame, Mona bowls a strike, Brooklyn style. She gives Johnny a playful, sarcastic smile and then flips him off, mouthing the words "fuck off." This flusters him, and he bowls himself into a 7-10 split.

"I can pick that up for you, Sport," Bruce yells, and the crowd laughs.

Johnny takes care of the 7-pin but leaves the 10-pin standing like a lone soldier after a long battle.

They approach the tenth frame and the anchor bowlers for each team in the final game. The "X-Men" lead by one pin in the game and by one point in the match. Jennifer Reynolds bowls first and gets three strikes to finish strong. She returns to her team's area and gives Billy a cold, piercing stare. He found it hot for a second and then shook his head at the thought of him hooking up with one of the Reynolds. He does his traditional shimmy, which makes the ladies giggle before he rolls his shiny rock. The pins collapse for Billy's first strike.

After another strike by the "X-Men's" best player, it's down to his final roll on lane 24. A strike by Billy and the "X-Men" will take the championship. However, another strike will also give Billy his first 300 game, which has been eluding him his whole life. He shimmies, struts down the lane, and releases the ball from his grip. Again, as time slowed, we watched the shiny blue metallic colored ball approach the helpless ten white pins. Everyone appears to be holding their breathes. After the ball strikes the pins ferociously, a loud thunderous crash fills the silent "Bowl-A-Frama" air.

The wobbling 10-pin from days of long ago returns to mock Billy. All eyes are on the swaying drunken 10-pin, and everyone's trying to impose goodwill on it to tumble to the floor. Billy gives the laughing 10-pin a sinister smile when he realizes it's about to tumble over and send his team to the Olympic regionals. He turns to his rivals and gives them the "game over bitches" look. The 10-pin hitting the floor is the last sound heard before the roaring cheers from everyone besides the Reynolds in the building.

"You did it, Billy! I'll stake your shoes back as soon as possible and put them somewhere special, no rush!" Peter yells from the front desk, holding two pairs of women's size 7 rental shoes close to his nose.

Through the crowd, Billy sees Stella standing in the back, watching the entire time. She gives him the most incredible smile he's ever seen. This is the moment, and he confidently walks over in her direction. Understanding what is happening, Bobby gives Billy a pat on the back for encouragement. The crowd parts the way and creates a path for Billy to reach Stella.

"Way to go, Mr. Billy. That was truly impressive," Stella says in her irresistible Russian accent that Billy has locked into his brain.

He goes in for a hug and kiss. She quickly puts her arms up to stop him.

"What are you doing, Mr. Billy?" she says, putting a screeching halt to the vibe.

Billy and everyone watching realize that he completely misread the situation. Stella still gives him a flirtatious smile.

"Mr. Billy, I said that was impressive. But if you want a kiss and hug from me, you'll have to go up there and bowl another strike. If you miss, I hug and kiss Bruce instead," she announces.

"Hell yeah, sorry, Billy!" Bruce yells out.

Billy grabs his blue metallic ball once more. He stares down at the 10 pins, awaiting his rounded wingman. He takes a deep breath before approaching the bowling ball carousal.

"Don't worry, you'll miss it and go home alone to jack off at what could have been, loser," Jeremy Reynolds says as he passes.

Billy picks up his trusty sidekick and takes a few calming, deep breaths. Of all the bowling balls he's released down the lanes over the years, this one is the most important of all time.

He does his shimmy, and Stella gives a smile he can't see but strangely feels. A wave of calmness comes over him, and he approaches the foul line to release his blue metallic wingman. The ball is traveling the same path it did moments ago when he clinched the championship, the perfect game, and a trip to the regionals. He smirks, knowing he'll kiss and hug Stella in a few seconds.

Crash! The pins appear to explode and quickly get swallowed into the ball pit... Well, except for one all-to-familiar wobbling and laughing 10-pin. Billy's calm feeling is replaced with anxiety while helplessly watching the fate of his first kiss with Stella reside on that demon 10-pin. Once again, everyone, except for the Reynolds, wishes for that pin to surrender.

This time, the 10-pin snuggles back to his upright position on the pin table, and the crowd moans in disappointment.

"Told ya loser. Whack it tonight!" Jeremy breaks the awkward silence.

Even the Reynolds, except Jeremy, actually felt bad for him. Everyone was so focused on the 10-pin's fate that they didn't notice that Stella had walked up to Billy and was standing behind him. Billy turned around with his head slightly downward in disappointment. He nearly ran right into Stella before noticing her legs. He gave her a look of confusion and excitement.

"That's a strike in 9-pin bowling," she says before leaning in for a kiss.

ABOUT THE AUTHOR

Self-proclaimed world-famous author Lance Hyden, with over 65 million words sold, was built on the assembly lines in the mean, or better yet, high-spirited streets of Detroit, Michigan. Starting his high school years during the best decade ever... the 80s, he would trade the miserable cold snowy days of the Midwest for a much cheerful warmer sunny Southwest climate by moving to Phoenix, Arizona with his father. After graduating from high school...barely, he enlisted in the United States Marine Corp, easy ladies he's married. He served his beloved country during the Gulf War and Los Angeles riots, you're welcome! Once his time in the Marines came to end, he moved from the beautiful California west coast back to the gloomy grey skies of Michigan, what a dumbass, to attend Eastern Michigan University and earned a bachelor's degree in Film. However, during his 4 years of college, the warmth of the west kept calling him back, or maybe it was the frozen snot from his nose telling him to leave. Only a couple of months after walking across the stage receiving his bachelor's diploma...barely, he moved back to Phoenix with some college friends. He now resides in Mesa, Arizona at the Hyden Hideaway with his beautiful Welsh wife, Deb, and their combined 4 boys (Carter, Preston, Ben, and Jacob). He has a passion for meeting new people, delicious food and posh cocktails, movies, binge-watching tv shows, and writing stories...Duh! He enjoys day trips around Arizona and longer trips to Los Angeles, San Diego, and his favorite location Las Vegas whenever possible.

He has three published books; *Tales from the H1d3away*, *East Haven*, and *Tale Gate*. Also, three short stories published in a collection of short story books: *Irrational Fears, ODDisms,* and *Renegades of Prose* (all found on Amazon, shameless plug).

Please share your thoughts (good or bad, but good) and which story you enjoyed the best by contacting me at, lancehyden@gmail.com (easiest and preferred method), AuthorLanceHyden on Facebook, www.lancehyden.com, or www.amazon.com/stores/author/B0BG3DYRC4

Enjoy and Thank you!

Made in the USA
Columbia, SC
20 August 2024

40361671R00108